OR GET IN THE WAY!

Adventures in Corporate America

D. CHARLES GOSSMAN

OR GET IN THE WAY!
ADVENTURES IN CORPORATE AMERICA

iUniverse books may be ordered through booksellers or by contacting:

iUniverse
1663 Liberty Drive
Bloomington, IN 47403
www.iuniverse.com
844-349-9409

ISBN: 978-1-6632-3700-2 (sc)
ISBN: 978-1-6632-3701-9 (hc)
ISBN: 978-1-6632-4022-4 (e)

Library of Congress Control Number: 2022910026

Print information available on the last page.

iUniverse rev. date: 07/05/2022

PREFACE

Haven't we *already* identified all possible leadership concepts, documented them in popular management books, and put them on hundreds of shelves (or web sites) for any prospective manager to study? Haven't we also developed entirely new management techniques while forcing ourselves to become experts at online meetings, remote teaching, and working from home using innovative internet apps? And doing all this while attempting to survive a multiyear pandemic featuring a Greek-alphabet soup of variants? These new challenges aren't causing unexpected new management issues, are they? Well, maybe. But are the fundamental leadership tenets still the same? Well, maybe!

Dan Graham believed he was educated in modern management thought as a young college hire, but he soon found he had missed a few lessons along the way. Today, just when we think we have harvested all the insights from tomes like Blanchard's One Minute Manager series or Goldratt's *The Goal* (not to mention a thousand other popular books), we are suddenly confronted with pandemic-driven management issues that were never even considered by contemporary researchers! Scientists can develop vaccinations to thwart unwanted infections, but can we ever develop an inoculation to counter toxic management or contaminated leadership? Well, not yet.

As a new hire, Dan's first supervisor warned him he could never excuse a poor performance by complaining that he was the victim of unenlightened leadership. Instead, he was goaded to greatness with the phrase "Keep your nose clean and do a good job, and you'll go right up in this company." Back then, everyone knew there must be more to it than that—and there is more to it today as well, especially in these uncertain times. When your supervisors have only seen your two-dimensional image on a laptop screen and have never even occupied the same room, you just might have a tough time convincing them to check the box "Promotable Now" next to your name.

These days, it is profoundly difficult to keep your career on that upward trajectory when you are relegated to remote video meetings. But that problem is not exactly a new one. We also observed it when late twentieth-century businesses implemented reengineering projects that fundamentally reorganized entire corporations. Dan Graham first saw this remote management dilemma when many supervisors suddenly found their employees relocated hundreds of miles away, and that *was before* the convenience of a half-dozen apps for video web meetings! Dan will forever remember the response his human resources department suggested when his subordinates complained their work locations were to be relocated hundreds of miles from their homes. "We don't tell you where to live. We just tell you where to report to work next Monday!"

Successfully leading during those types of upheavals certainly made it easier to add nice entries on one's resume, but there are many other factors that impact a career as well. In fact, one element we can never ignore is *luck*, and Dan was no stranger to that either. We can all acknowledge that competence and confidence are essential, but *luck*—that serendipitous notion that you must be in the *right place at the right time*—is often important for advancement too. Dan Graham's corporate career featured several episodes that can only be described that way. Unfortunately, those events were often quite costly to close friends and coworkers who found themselves on the opposite side of that *luck*. I certainly acknowledged this in my career, and a good portion of the book that follows explores this idea as well.

Dan always insisted that acknowledging the role of luck did not imply that hard work and "stick-to-it-iveness" were a wasted effort, but he always questioned why so many hardworking and deserving people simply did not rise to become executives, social media darlings, or high-profile billionaires. I, too, have thought long and hard about this condition and have concluded that you should not be labeled a failure simply because you weren't lucky enough to reach 100,000 subscribers on your social media accounts!

But what about this old saying attributed to Thomas Jefferson: "The harder I work the luckier I get"? That is certainly a well-intentioned axiom that encourages honest effort rather than idle behavior. Nonetheless, it always seems disingenuous when an immensely successful person attributes their lofty position solely to hard work and a "never give up" attitude. They conveniently forget to mention that they were lucky enough to inherit some start-up funding from Uncle Leo or fortunate enough to have parents who permitted them to live at home until they were thirty-three as they grew their business. They also ignore the fact that, as successful entrepreneurs, they enjoyed the good fortune (read that *luck)* of finding a lucrative business niche that no one had exploited before. *Hmmm.* Isn't that suspiciously like saying they were *lucky to be in the right place at the right time?* Looking back on all this, Dan thought so!

This book is a collection of fictional short stories based on my experiences during a multidecade corporate career. Of course, the names were changed to "protect the innocent." When recounting these stories as I prepared this manuscript, I realized that many of the lessons I learned were actually interesting examples of the theories and teachings found in basic college management courses. There was clearly no intention of summarizing any formal *learning outcomes* in these episodes. That is better left to the scholars preparing academic texts. Instead, most of these are presented with the intention of bringing a slight smile to the reader. On the other hand, there are subtle lessons in each story that might guide up-and-coming managers in how to react in similar business situations. To that end, I have summarized a few of the concepts in a couple of indexes at the end of this book. Index 1 offers an alphabetized list of business, leadership, and management topics indexed by chapter number. Index

2 is a simple listing of the business, leadership, and management topics discussed in each chapter.

This effort is not intended to offer an exhaustive compendium of management thought over the last century, but it should serve as an elementary introduction, or *study guide*, to some of the issues still faced by managers in contemporary companies. I'm not sure Dan Graham had all these concepts categorized in his mind during his career, but I *can* be sure he wouldn't care if I shared them with you now!

D. Charles Gossman
March 2022

ACKNOWLEDGMENTS

A special thanks to my wife, Eve, daughter, Kellie, and son, Matt, who contributed proofreading and constructive criticism as I prepared several versions of this manuscript over a dozen years.

Having started a second career in academics after retiring from my first in the corporate arena, I have enjoyed half a century of observing (and learning from) bosses, employees, colleagues, students, and family. As I reflect on these people, I am fortunate that many helped (and are still helping) to shape my life. I can look back and certainly acknowledge the role my parents had in raising me, but I also recognize the profound influence Eve has had as well.

Finally, more in keeping with the purpose of this note, I could never ignore the influences of my working relationships in forming the person I've become. Although the characters in this book are entirely fabricated, many were loosely called to mind by those I worked with over the years. To all who influenced me, positively or negatively, I extend a heartfelt thank-you!

INTRODUCTION

Some say that the phrase "Lead, follow, or get *out* of the way" originated with Founding Father Thomas Paine, so I guess that sentiment has been around for a long time. The old adage is usually quoted by some no-nonsense leader who intends to push through all the obstacles (reluctant workers or other barriers) to succeed at all costs. What Thomas (and many subsequent leaders) failed to realize is that there is actually a fourth choice in the leadership equation. Sometimes, as a few leaders eventually come to understand, you simply have to "get *in* the way!" That realization floats to the surface when leaders confront some impediment that *doesn't* get out of the way so easily. They are often arrogant enough to think their past triumphs are predictive of future successes, but those previous experiences may be the result of coincidence, luck, or some wholly unrelated reason. That's when they suddenly realize their leadership traits are based on misconceptions, misunderstandings, or downright unsupported myths! Fortunately, Dan Graham started learning this lesson as a small child.

Until he was four or five years old, baby boomer Dan Graham was certain he was the luckiest boy in the world. When old enough to dress and put on his shoes, Dan's mom guided him in selecting the right shoe for the right foot and the left shoe for the left foot. The learning process took several days of reinforcement, but he soon got it right.

Eventually, while practicing that daily routine of slipping on shoes (and tying them—another triumph for a youngster), he realized he had not paid much attention to the socks. Then it dawned on him: he always seemed to get the right sock on the right foot the first time! He never experienced the discomfort of forcing a foot into the wrong sock as he did when mismatching a left shoe with a right foot. He deduced, based on the experimental data collected over months of checking each time he put on his socks, that he got it right the first time, every time, time after time. He assumed he was just darned lucky. In fact, he assumed he was the luckiest kid in the world. Just think about what that insight did for Dan's self-esteem and sense of well-being! All the same, he simply failed to grasp the significance of this "feat with the feet."

Then, one day, Dan made the mistake of mentioning the lucky streak to his mom and learned the truth. With a knowing chuckle, she revealed that it didn't matter which sock you placed on the left and right because they would always feel OK.

It was at this precise moment that Dan formulated a set of fundamental but daunting truths. Well, perhaps he did not piece together all the facts at that time, but looking back on that experience while a young manager in a major corporation, he outlined the axioms revealed that day.

- Conditions are not always as good or as bad as thought.
- One rarely has all the data to make informed decisions.
- Now and then, people will operate successfully in an environment in which they have wholly misjudged basic facts.
- Sometimes, a crushing revelation about long-held beliefs will shake a person's confidence to the core—or *not!*
- Unfounded optimism is an excellent mode of operation in life until reality confronts a person. Unfortunately, the wide-eyed optimist sometimes fails to recognize the necessity for contingencies *and suffers the consequences!*
- And finally, never underestimate the supremacy of *plain old luck!*

One can infer a final observation from Dan's story. Life experiences, no matter how simplistic they seem, can offer insights into one's psyche, interpersonal relationships, business transactions, and even leadership traits. In fact, fateful experiences can help to structure successful life philosophies as managers learn from positive outcomes while discarding those that prove unconstructive.

Scholars, searching for truths like these, turn to the life experience of business leaders for inspiration. These lessons often help to refine the underlying theories and shore up popular authors who describe them to the masses. A few even retain the mistaken perception that real-world managers cannot succeed unless the next book guides them to greatness. They think leaders feel helpless until they read and apply the strategies outlined in the next popular management theory found in the *Seven Steps to Outstanding Leadership* or some other equally auspicious title. But as suggested here, quite the opposite may be true. The management authors rarely invent management strategies; they often simply observe the good managers in business and attempt to explain why they are effective. Perhaps managers cannot describe their practices in the theoretical jargon of scientific research, but many experienced supervisors have based their management style on sound practices, whether they realize it or not.

No, a good leader does not wait until theorists describe effective methods he or she might adopt. Blanchard's *One Minute Manager*, for example, describes the process much the way it really happens. That usually involves managers developing a style using trial and error over the years and finding *when* it works very well. They then invite others to learn why the style works so well. Afterward, a researcher comes along to advance a theory and invites speculation on *why* it is effective.

Researchers Bass and Stogdill, for example, described some 3,000 studies in their 1981 leadership handbook edition. Nearly three decades later, however, over 8,000 published research articles were featured in the 1,500 pages of their fourth edition. So what do these statistics suggest? Merely that there are thousands upon thousands of management and leadership practices. Some are effective, some are not, and some are probably based on entirely bogus research. So why does so much research in management and leadership appear to be contradictory? Possibly because researchers express a bit of bias or subtle data manipulation as they develop their methodologies. As the noted psychology researcher Brian Nosek suggests, "There is no cost to getting things wrong. The cost is not getting them [scientific studies] published."

Thus, it is always wise to reserve the right to challenge any truths discovered in all these thousands of studies. Many of them focus exclusively on the importance of completing tasks; others contradict this by asserting that we should pay more attention to developing employee-supervisor relationships. Still others insist on the importance of combining the best of both. Unfortunately, popular authors tend to selectively cite from these suspect or sensational studies as they promise to "reveal the truly hidden secrets to great leadership" or some such hokum.

For better or worse, this seems to offer a cafeteria approach to management theory. Fortunately, most leaders do not actually push a tray through this virtual lunchroom of topics, selecting from rules of thumb on the top shelf, traditional wisdom on the shelf to the left, and the prepackaged lessons from previous managers at the checkout register. A boss planning to feast on a plate piled high with a mashup of theories from the research du jour surely faces a rude awakening! Regardless of their personal understanding of motivation, personality, behaviors, leader traits, or worker characteristics, business leaders were out there every day managing and leading long before some researcher came along to study their efforts.

The short stories in this book loosely relate to some of the management and leadership lessons Dan Graham gleaned from his supervisors over the years. Some of their practices were supported by solid leadership theory and research, and some were not. Many of his managers had effective leadership skills but lacked the ability to explain the underlying hypotheses they employed. As Dan came to realize, real leaders are people who find some form of success and then teach others by sharing their insights. Sometimes that is positive, and sometimes it is negative. He also learned a great deal from those managers who forced him to get *out of their way* when he was hindering progress. But most importantly, he came to recognize when to ignore all the management theorists and, sometimes, simply "get *in* the way!" Personally, I'm not sure, but perhaps there is some fundamental truth in that approach to leadership. That is for *you* to decide!

1

It's Not Rocket Science

In the late 1960s and early 1970s, Dan Graham's telecommunications company met growth needs by identifying top nonmanagement technicians with ten or fifteen years of experience and promoted them into the engineering management ranks. They were generally experienced in the appropriate disciplines and continued their careers as nonsupervisory managers with the word "engineer" in their new job title. The company did not require a professional engineering certification, much less a degree in engineering, to hold these jobs. The corporation subjected the newly promoted workers to several hundred hours of schooling to ready them for capital-cost economics, computer applications, supervision and management, and a dozen other engineering subjects. After many weeklong training sessions, usually at a distant corporate training center, they were ready to take on the role of qualified field engineers in their company.

At that time, the South Florida housing industry was in a high growth mode with the rapid development of subdivisions. Census data details a doubling of Florida's population from 1970 to 1995 and much of the increase centered in the southeastern counties. The company had difficulty promoting enough field engineers from internal applicants, so it began to look outside the company to attract graduates from engineering colleges. The firm recruited engineers at campus job fairs and became active in university internship programs to attract and retain more.

Dan Graham interviewed at a campus job fair and received an offer for employment at the region's telecom giant. College engineers earned a $10,000 salary and held the entry-level title junior engineer. They also endured all the additional training that other internally promoted engineers received while avoiding the lengthy on-the-job investment. There was some jealousy and perhaps animosity because these youngsters skipped to the top "without paying their dues." After a few months of good-natured teasing, coupled with some positive working relationships, these concerns began to subside.

Soon, a new problem emerged for the recently promoted and newly hired engineers: competition from NASA! To put this in perspective, Dan's hectic year included graduation on June 4, 1972, reporting to work on June 5, 1972, and attending his wedding on June 24, 1972. This was also an eventful year as NASA's final Apollo moon mission launched on December 7, 1972. At first, the end of the moon missions did not have much impact on the company's engineering workforce. To be sure, some former NASA engineers and contractors had recognized the warning signs early on and sought work outside the space program. Dan's employer was already casually picking up stray engineers from the space race and a few had advanced quickly, becoming staff managers or supervising engineers. When the space project finally concluded in December of Graham's first year, however, the number of experts looking for work in Florida exploded. Numerous contractors and subcontractors, such as IBM, Grumman, Boeing, TRW, Rockwell, and hundreds of others, faced the consequences.

At its pinnacle, History.com suggests that NASA's workforce reached 34,000 employees supported by another 375,000 industry contractors. Obviously, thousands of engineers were looking for jobs by early 1973. Like a horde of locusts, these highly qualified engineers—genuine *rocket scientists*—descended on Dan's company. When the best candidates were hired, most of Graham's peers realized that their career advancement plans had come to an immediate halt. Certainly, they could not fault their company's HR department for hiring a highly qualified workforce with advanced degrees at one-fifth their former salary. But unfortunately, the company was no longer interested in internally promoting field engineers or hiring recent college graduates. The existing field-engineering workforce collectively realized that most of these new personnel would quickly fill all the higher management roles. Competing with real rocket scientists for future promotions seemed a futile option for an inexperienced college graduate.

It turned out, however, that this windfall of talent did *not* develop into the productive workforce envisioned by human resources. Established company engineers mocked the new hires as clueless "space cadets." Some did studies with subtexts suggesting they were difficult to motivate because they were "launching moon missions one day, planting telephone poles the next!" It was clear that for the majority of these new hires, telecommunications engineering was not only beneath their dignity but also beneath their paygrade and salary expectations. One long-term telecom engineer always spoke of the moon men with contempt, calling them "those guys with *'E's* after their name." He explained that they always ended their correspondence with acronyms such as *BSEE, MSEE, IEEE, PE,* or *IIE,* all of which were various engineering degrees, certifications, or professional memberships. It was a common way they underscored their superior education and background. They were truly overqualified, underutilized, and underpaid based on their resumes.

To be sure, many of the overqualified engineers left the company as soon as other opportunities came along. Other older rocket men remained only to finish their careers as unmotivated, miserable telecom engineers. Nevertheless, the existing field engineers competed with a significant number of aggressive, competent ex-rocket scientists in their early forties who quickly earned supervisory positions. The less flashy but more experienced internal workforce accepted its fate, understanding they had lost any chance for future advancement.

To motivate some of the younger engineers, supervisors began using the phrase "Keep your nose clean and do a good job, and you will get promoted before you know it!" To some degree, this encouragement was still true after the influx of the moon men. In the early 1970s, the company still subscribed to a vertical hierarchical organization featuring multiple levels within every job position. In theory, you *could* earn a promotion, just not a promotion to a supervisory position. For example, HR designed the first-level engineering organization chart to include steps starting with the entry-level junior engineer, then assistant engineer, associate engineer, (full) engineer, and finally senior engineer. None of these titles had supervisory responsibilities so all were simply steps in the progression to a supervising engineer. A supervising engineer typically managed a group of fifteen or twenty personnel, but that position was about as high in the company as most of these managers could ever realize. The engineers at that time understood that if they "kept their noses clean and did a good job," they could indeed receive that next promotion—with commensurate salary increase—at predictable intervals.

Soon after the rocket boys touched down, however, HR dismantled that five-step system. Instead, all first-level management employees with the word "engineer" in their job title became, simply, engineers. Consequently, a reclassified junior engineer could never again ascend multiple steps and pay raises before achieving that desired supervisor title. To their credit, the HR department recognized the demotivating aspect of this change and acknowledged to the entire first-level management workforce that it would be forever *plateaued*—a euphemism for *no more promotions*—until a supervisory opening popped up. Unfortunately, when that happened, they were competing with hundreds of other *plateaued* individuals. Then HR found an even more innovative way to deal with the motivational problems. While acknowledging that very few would ever achieve the next level, they suggested returning to college, while working full time, for an undergraduate or advanced degree like an MBA or PhD. The company had an excellent tuition program, thus successfully encouraging many to take this path. While temporarily keeping their minds off their stalled careers, HR had overlooked the fact that those shiny new degrees failed to open new opportunities in the company. With no place to go, they would remain trapped in the quagmire. The morale problems continued.

Graham completed his graduate degrees and faced the same problem, convinced he would remain a first-level engineer forever. Only an official vacancy above Dan would permit a promotion, and then hundreds of other qualified and deserving first-level engineering managers—including rocket scientists—would be vying for the position as well.

Dan was always amused that "next in line" employees felt insulted when passed over for promotions. They believed in a utopian universe wherein upper management would constantly scan the deserving masses before magically anointing and appointing the best and brightest to the next higher slot on the org chart. Reporting to John Voorhees in District Engineer "Cy" Greene's territory, Dan knew it *never* worked that way. He understood workplace politics and the three conditions necessary for advancement.

1. A manager must have achieved some attention due to reputation and/or accomplishments.
2. The manager must have secured a sponsor or mentor willing to recommend or request him or her to fill a supervisory *slot.*
3. That organizational *slot* must pop open.

He had met the first two conditions relatively early in his career and was waiting patiently for the third when he heard rumors from staff supervisor Ron Whitman that he (Dan) was in the running for a great job in Ron's prestigious area transmission staff. It was not a promotion, but many considered it a conspicuous stepping-stone to a future supervisory job.

After his transfer to the area staff, Graham continued to perform as a first level with high-profile responsibilities, but the supervisory landscape remained bare. Reporting to Whitman, he served on a team with several ex-NASA workers who were similarly determined and deserving of achieving career success as well. He worked directly with Robert Harrel, a senior engineer hired away from the airline industry. Robert's unique knowledge fit nicely into the telecommunications industry, and few of the company's workers were qualified in that niche. Dan knew he needed to learn all he could about the subject, abiding by the old adage that one should always attempt to make himself indispensable—or at least difficult to replace.

Having been a former air force officer, Harrell joined the reserves about that time, all the while knowing that several of his fellow reservists were skydivers. As expected, Robert rejoined the sport he enjoyed years earlier. Owing to their daily working relationship, Dan and Robert often shared dinner outings and events with their families, but Harrell could never convince Graham to join him in that exciting recreational activity.

Everyone on the staff was shocked to learn that Robert Harrell, the young father of a toddler, died in a skydiving accident later that year. Nevertheless, the shock and mourning period did not last long before desperately ambitious staff engineers were lining up to fill Robert's senior position. Unfortunately, the company had created a system that placed a premium on the misfortune of anyone holding a higher-level position. Employees did not publicly wish harm on anyone, but many seemed secretly pleased whenever a higher employee fell by the wayside, whether by misfortune, misconduct, or any other event that created a vacancy in the org chart. Too close to the situation, Graham attempted to distance himself from the process by staying focused on concluding the responsibilities he and Harrell had shared.

Several weeks passed before Whitman announced Dan's promotion to backfill the slot. Graham's peers were secretly disappointed, but most understood the reasoning as Graham was the only active staff member capable of absorbing Robert's workload. Graham found it an unsettling experience but made the best of the situation. The most unnerving revelation was that the new corporate advancement strategy literally hinged on the death of a senior member. Each manager seemed to realize that his or her career strategies and plans had changed forever.

Within a year, Whitman accepted a rotational assignment, one of the few promotional opportunities remaining in the company. Ron had discovered that if a supervisor was willing to relocate his or her family to global headquarters some 1,500 miles away, a promotion to the third level of management might follow within two years back in the home state. That was assuming the home state could also "manufacture" an opening, a not-so-sure probability in those years. Nevertheless, since only one in a thousand reached that *district manager* title, Ron found it worth the effort. Fortunately, the plans played out nicely and Ron returned to lead a newly formed field engineering district.

Whitman inherited several older, experienced supervising engineers in his new district, and all went well for a year. As a relatively young district manager (and former drill instructor in the Marine Corps), Ron was capable of handling the stress inherent in the new job. Some of his older supervisors were not. In fact, his most experienced supervisor, Bud Mitchell, suffered a major heart attack during a particularly stressful project-scheduling meeting. As the EMTs loaded him into the ambulance, Bud guaranteed Ron that he would soon be back on the job and stronger than ever. After quadruple bypass surgery, Mitchell's condition weakened, and he never returned to work. Whitman's callous division manager, Burt Larkin, ordered Whitman to "find a younger guy who won't die on the job." Whitman began the search for Bud's replacement.

Remaining on Steve McKinney's area staff, Graham had continued providing technical support throughout the region after his direct supervisor (Whitman) had departed a few years earlier. McKinney was the proverbial high achiever, already holding an important executive position while still in his early thirties. Graham always felt that McKinney, an intimidating leader, underestimated anyone with a less aggressive leadership style, and Dan was certainly in that category. So Graham was both surprised and relieved to receive Ron's call one Tuesday afternoon.

"Hi, Danny. I guess you heard about Bud a couple of months ago. Well, he won't be back with us. You'll report to me next Monday in the South Engineering District. You are replacing Bud as my new support manager. Your promotion will be official in a week."

Graham realized his job as a newly minted supervisor, at twenty-nine years of age, would be especially challenging. He was one of only two or three supervising engineers under the age of thirty in the entire company's engineering department. When he met his new workforce, he began to grasp the trial he was facing. His finance manager was a new hire with very little project budgeting experience. The company had recently promoted his lead administrative supervisor from the district's pool of clerical employees. Not only was she younger than several of the more experienced clerks, but many of her former peers were also openly hostile. In the sexist corporate world of the early 1980s, her assessment program evaluator's primary endorsement centered on the comment that the young woman had "very expressive eyes." Other important personnel on Graham's support team were former field engineers transferred to Whitman's district. These were supposed to be specialists who would resolve customer service complaints, qualified project managers, administrators with telecom construction expertise, and budgeting experts. When Larkin ordered his division directors to help staff the new district, Whitman's "helpful" peers instead transferred all their less-than-productive employees. The staffing practice fooled no one; it was simply standard procedure for Larkin's division—a division that thrived on constant competition instead of teamwork.

After he was on the job for about three months, Dan received a call from a disabled Bud Mitchell who had finally filed his retirement papers after thirty-nine years on the job. He explained that a friend offered transportation to the building so he could recover his personal belongings. Six months earlier, his former employees collected and placed them in a large storage box labeled "Bud's stuff" and stacked it on a shelf in the storage room. It rested for several months on that shelf next to the district's standard supplies: pencils, pens, paper pads, graphical drawing tools, and so forth. When Dan escorted Bud to the room, they initially had some trouble finding it. Someone had relocated it to a top shelf with the label pointing toward the wall. After a few minutes of searching, Graham pulled the box from the shelf and placed it on the small table in the middle of the room. It was nearly empty, containing a few business cards, a couple of used pens and pencils, and a paper pad reflecting the final meeting notes recorded before the ambulance ride. All other materials, files, and personal belongings had disappeared, presumably pilfered by employees who needed supplies or information during the last six months. Bud peered into the box in disbelief. Dan turned away as he noticed tears welling up in Bud's eyes. As he dumped the contents into a small paper bag, he turned back to his twenty-nine-year-old successor and lamented, "You work your whole life, and this is all you have to show for it."

Nearly three years after Dan reported to the South District, the corporate grapevine suggested that headquarters planned to downsize Whitman's district after surviving their "certification" program. That program involved an intense efficiency analysis that typically ended with a recommendation for a workforce reduction. Graham knew that the company would target at least one of the four supervising engineers as well. As fate would have it, Dan had relocated his family to the northernmost of the three counties in his region a mere two months before Ron promoted him in their southernmost county. A round trip of over one hundred miles a day seemed worth it for the promotion at first. After a couple of years, the daily travel, leaving at 5 a.m. and returning at 8 p.m. six days a week, was getting old. Dan saw an opportunity for a lateral transfer as a supervisor in the new regional technical support staff located just a few miles from his home, solving both the downsizing problem and the travel issue. Dan was a bit surprised at how quickly District Manager Sam Rendell extended an invitation for a visit after receiving Graham's inquiry. Upon arriving, Dan was ushered into a large office full of boxes.

"If you agree to transfer, this is where you will be seated," Sam explained. "By the way, all these boxes contain Jim Heron's files and personal effects. He died of lung cancer last month and we need to replace him as soon as possible." Dan transferred to yet another important job in his career.

Dan had served in Whitman's engineering district under Larkin for three years. The management lessons were numerous, but most centered on how *not* to manage people. Larkin's monthly divisional meetings became infamous throughout the company, so much so that Graham was a minor celebrity when he transferred to the new staff position after serving time in the South District. His typical introductions concluded with "You worked for Burt Larkin? How did you survive? That must have been just awful …"

Looking back on his first few years at that point, he knew that competence and confidence were the *givens* for a solid career, but he also realized there were other conditions necessary for advancement. He recited the list to himself: gathering attention through accomplishments, finding a respected sponsor, and enjoying enough luck to be in the right place at the right time (i.e., inheriting an open position). He was living proof that the popular philosophy *I did it my way* was rarely accurate. Graham would never forget that corporate careers rarely materialize without a Steve McKinney or a Ron Whitman, and unfortunately, many young managers would not enjoy an upwardly mobile career without a Robert Harrell, a Bud Mitchell, or a Jim Heron. He learned in the most uncomfortable manner that if you were lucky enough to earn a promotion, there was likely some poor, unlucky colleague who paid the price and had to *get out of the way!* Contemplating all these perplexing feelings, he thought, *Welcome to corporate America!*

2

Twelve Ducks, One Tuck, and Three Squirrels

R. L. "Cy" Greene attended South Carolina's Furman University on a baseball scholarship—and he earned his nickname. As a pitcher, everyone assumed the term was a reference to Cy Young, the famous player for whom the annual best major league pitcher award was named. Greene enjoyed the comparison and never corrected anyone when discussing the origin of his nickname. However, Graham learned years later that it was not, in fact, a reference to his pitching expertise. Instead, he received it when his coach replaced him in the third inning of a championship game. He walked three batters, on four balls each, throwing every pitch so high that the batters had to duck as the ball sailed up and over their heads. When his coach finally pulled him from the game, he said, "Greene, I can't have you throwing at the sky out there anymore today. Hit the bench. You're out." His teammates heard the "sky" comment and immediately began calling him "Sky" Greene throughout the remainder of his playing days. Later, Green himself refashioned the name into *Cy* as a more fitting moniker for a not-quite-good-enough ballplayer.

Greene never entirely stopped playing baseball, at least in his mind. He still practiced the gestures he once used in his baseball career. If he stopped for a moment to speak to someone in the hall, he would solidly tap the floor with the toe of his shoe behind his opposite leg. He would then complete that action with the other shoe. It was the same subconscious motion he used twenty years earlier to expel the red clay from his baseball cleats. Sometimes, he assumed a baseball pitcher's set or stretch position, a sideways stance on the mound. He employed that as a nineteen-year-old pitcher, using only peripheral vision to detect a runner stealing second base. Similarly, Cy would stand sideways and turn to face the person he was addressing, all the while appearing to look for runners trying to steal on him. It was an unnerving experience.

A shy, young man, Dan reported to work on his first day promptly at 8:25 a.m. for an 8:30 a.m. start time. Walking through the door for the first time, he looked for the district engineer's office and found R. L. "Cy" Greene's door to the immediate right. Mr. Greene, a relatively inexperienced district manager promoted out of South Carolina's accounting department, spoke with the heavy drawl one would expect. Graham knocked lightly on the open door and announced, "Hello. I'm Dan Graham, the new guy."

As Greene extended his hand for a firm handshake, he spoke loudly so the outer office personnel could hear, "Daniel, boy, you got banker's hours already?" When Cy pronounced the word *boy*, as he often referred to his young engineers, it came out sounding like *boa*. Graham quickly learned his first lesson about the culture at the telecom: arrive at work an hour early and stay an hour late.

Dan's second lesson on culture came a few weeks later when Cy approached Jules, one of the other young engineers, and ordered him to clear his desk before leaving for the day. Since the engineering job required a great deal of reference materials and large informational maps called plats, most of the youngsters left everything on their desk so they could get quickly started the next day. Mr. Greene would have none of it. Jules, a young engineer with an advanced degree, did not appreciate the order and argued his position. After a few minutes behind closed doors, the young man left Greene's office and announced that he had turned in his resignation. Greene exited his office a few minutes later and assured everyone that the young man would be back. He then, more politely, asked a couple of the older engineers to clear the young man's desk and refile the materials. Jules, the young father of two, came in two days later and requested to resume his job. He returned to his desk after his emotional apology. Jules maintained an immaculate desk for the rest of his career. Dan did as well.

A third lesson surfaced a year later. The company had excellent benefits in those days, and the young engineers earned two full weeks of vacation after a year. Since Dan had skipped his honeymoon when he married just nineteen days after reporting to work, he casually mentioned to Mr. Greene early in his second year that he would soon take his two-week vacation. "Daniel, boy, you need to realize if I can do without you for two weeks, I can do *without* you." Graham changed his plans and declined consecutive weeks of vacation for the remainder of his career.

In the years before the Justice Department abolished monopolistic phone service, local telecoms focused on providing landlines to residential and business customers. A quarter of a century before cell phones were common, nearly everyone had one or two old-fashioned black telephones in their home. With the extensive subdivision development at that time, however, the company delayed many orders for weeks or months as the field engineers failed to keep up with the fast pace. Stacks of held service orders, issued on yellow, five-inch by seven-inch forms, found their way to every engineer's office while their supervisors demanded immediate attention. It was commonplace for a service job—extending phone cables several miles from a central office to the customer's home—to take three months for completion. The state's public service commission made sure the company remained focused on the problem as they controlled the company's revenue rates. Adding new engineers seemed the only solution to getting the problem under control.

Graham's direct supervisor, John Voorhees, placed Dan with a team of more experienced engineers when he first reported to the district as a newly hired junior engineer. Voorhees was a nondegreed supervisor who had worked his way up from a nonmanagement position. John's local field engineers maintained geographic areas with the assistance of drafting clerks who prepared their engineering blueprints from field notes. They specified cable types and locations, telephone pole types and locations, legal rights of way and easement authorizations, and so forth. The working drawings also contained detailed cost estimates for material and labor along with complex diagrams and symbols to instruct cable splicers how to connect several miles of wires, with the correct telephone number, directly to the customer awaiting telephone service. When these local field engineers (called distribution engineers in telecom parlance) gained years of experience, supervisors selected the best to learn the special engineering for *trunking* cable projects. Trunking cables carried digitized phone traffic between cities and states and the projects were significantly more costly and complex. Dan hoped to one day graduate from his distribution engineering role to earn a position in his district's elite trunking group.

After a few months of working with the field engineers, John assigned a "trial" territory to Dan, allowing him to handle all engineering in that region. The assignment involved "babysitting" telephone facilities in a suburban area of about five square miles. His charge was making sure 20,000 customers could expect a telephone installation within three days of their order. Graham found the job daunting but soon latched onto the concept, taking his wife on Sunday afternoon excursions to survey his engineered jobs under construction by the district crews. The newlywed's wife always expressed polite interest as she gazed upon a meaningless mass of tangled cables and splice cases nestled in open pits.

One day early in this new assignment, a road crew severed four major trunking cables in Dan's serving area, disconnecting phone service from about 10,000 customers. When Greene received the call on the outage, he called Voorhees, who immediately assigned Graham the task of preparing the repair project. Although it was actually a trunking project and Graham was only a local distribution engineer, he was the most expendable at the time since everyone else was busy "chasing service orders." The project had to include emergency engineering drawings and a budget package that headquarters would review and approve within twenty-four hours. The cable maintenance crews were making temporary repairs by laying huge cables on the sidewalks of a major highway, but they could not remain that way for more than a few days.

This would have been a relatively straightforward project for an experienced trunking engineer, but Dan had never submitted a job of that magnitude. Typically, a distribution engineer handled jobs in the $10,000 to $20,000 range (in 1970 dollars). This trunking cable project would cost well over $200,000 and require an exponential amount of supporting documentation. Obviously, Graham had no time to learn the process as Mr. Greene expected to review the initial paperwork in four hours when he returned to the office about noon. Voorhees gave him a few brief instructions, pulled a similar project from the district files, and told Dan to "make another one just like it, only different."

Dan made a quick visit to take field notes and measurements, returned to get the drafting clerks working on the drawings, and loaded budget data to a mainframe computer using their "state of the art" *punched-paper-tape* data entry system. When the teletype terminal finally rolled out the budget sheet, he asked the secretarial pool to start typing the funding approval paperwork. Since a project submittal of this magnitude required about ten copies for approval, typists prepared so-called stencils in an IBM Selectric typewriter. In the days prior to PCs, word processing, printers, and copiers, a person manually assembled these documents into a mimeograph machine that operated much like a miniature printing press. The project was coming together with three full-size (twenty-four-inch by thirty-six-inch) engineering drawings, a ten-page package of documents explaining the pricing and work content, plus material and labor printouts retrieved from the teletype machine.

Despite the effort, Dan was nowhere near completion when Cy rushed into the office before lunch and asked to review his progress. Seated behind an enormous desk placed in front of a sun-filled window, Dan was momentarily transfixed as he suddenly became aware of the aura radiating from Cy's head. Glinting off the sweat on that nearly hairless orb, Graham found himself attempting to count a dozen perfectly placed strands that Cy had fashioned across his bald spot.

Graham was abruptly summoned out of his trance when Cy began barking orders. Seeing that the project was still hours from completion, he directed Dan to "grab all the paperwork and bring it to my office." He closed the door and told Graham to spread the material out on his desk and take a seat in front of him. Greene quickly pointed out a couple of areas needing attention and additional detail and then said, *"Heldam,* Daniel my boy, you gotta understand this ain't no *eleemosynary* institute! We need to bill these boys some big bucks for tearin' up our cables."

Dan had never heard that "heldam" utterance before and had certainly never heard that other strange word: *eleemosynary.* As it turned out, Cy was a deeply religious man who could never bring himself to swear the oaths many in his profession had perfected years ago. So his unique go-to curse was heldam, a contraction of two common swear-words that, together, sounded slightly less offensive—at least in Cy's mind. But that other word had thrown everyone in the office for a loop. One of Dan's colleagues spent several hours the next day trying to find it in the dictionary. Cy had mispronounced it so badly that no one could spell it. Noting several *ee*'s near the beginning of the word, Greene had transposed them and mangled the pronunciation as *"eee-lah-mostinery."* When Graham's buddy finally figured out how to spell it, they realized it was simply a reference to a charitable organization. At that point, none of the young engineers in the group were convinced that Cy was a great leader, but they at least gave him credit for improving their vocabulary!

But back to Dan's trunking project. After receiving some quick advice on preparing the billing, Cy said, "Just sit here while you work on it. I'm here if you need me." Greene proceeded to handle his in-basket chores, eat his lunch, and take phone calls, completely ignoring Dan. As he exited and returned to Greene's office while collecting information, Graham kept thinking Greene would offer some additional guidance. Instead, he just kept asking, "How's it coming?" every thirty minutes. Then, after one final review, Greene added an insignificant note on the engineering drawings and signed the documents in seven or eight places. "Good. Now get it down to the division office before they close!"

After the ordeal, the other engineers wanted to know all the details. Had Cy yelled at Dan, had he berated his work, had he challenged the field notes? They also wanted to know if he had learned any other new words in the process! Dan found the experience hard to describe and, frankly, mystifying. Looking back, he realized Cy was expressing confidence—in his own way—by allowing Dan to attempt a very important job with little or no training. It started out as a very unnerving situation as Dan fully expected a micromanaged session with a boss looking directly over his shoulder every minute. It was not that at all. Greene understood that he did not need to be extremely directive but also knew that Dan needed to sense some level of support in that stressful situation. Cy filled the role well, becoming the helpful coach to the inexperienced player.

In retrospect, Dan realized he had not completed the project as efficiently as a more experienced engineer, but he was relieved that Coach Cy had not shouted at him, "Hit the bench! You're out!" as Greene's own baseball coach had done two decades earlier. At least, Graham thought, if that was a trial by fire, he had come through it with only a few minor burns!

Dan could never quite explain the experience to his fellow engineers. He simply told everyone, "All I'll say is you don't *ever* want it to happen to you!" Graham also made all his buddies promise to never use the words *heldam* or *eleemosynary* for as long as they worked together!

Not long after that incident, during a particularly hectic day with engineers busily working on held service orders, Voorhees called a team meeting. He explained that the engineering district was falling behind in their commitments. Rather than getting ahead of the service order problem, the totals were growing every day. It turned out that Graham's area, on the other hand, exhibited some of the better on-time results in the district. Dan was convinced this was due to his own engineering skills, but it was more likely due to the slower growth in his region. Secretly believing that John might point to him as the ideal example in their district, his thoughts drifted as he sat waiting for the official pat on the back. He knew it could be that first step in gaining an early promotion. Instead, Voorhees avoided compliments and simply announced he was reassigning Dan to maintain both his current area *plus* a portion of Tucker's adjacent area. The new area had much higher growth and a much higher held service rate. The others realized this was a veiled acknowledgment of Graham's accomplishments, but the "ceremony" was completely devoid of any public affirmation of his efforts.

A disappointed Graham thought about challenging Voorhees by suggesting it did not seem fair to have additional work heaped on him simply because he had better results than his peers did. He could not contain himself as he blurted out, "That feels like punishment. I'm going to be putting in even more hours to handle this new—"

Before he could finish, John ordered, "OK, Graham, run back down to your office and bring me a copy of the contract you signed when we hired you. We'll check on how to handle this right now."

Dan left the meeting and started down the hallway before realizing he had never seen a contract, much less signed one. Turning about halfway to his office, he walked slowly back into the room and said, "John, I don't think I ever signed a contract—"

Again cutting him off, Voorhees explained with a knowing grin, "Of course you didn't! You are a salaried, management employee! You have no contract with us. You're just another *dime-a-dozen* engineer and easily replaceable. And don't ever forget it!"

Dan found himself sharing the newly assigned area with "Tuck" Tucker. Since he only used initials before his last name, everyone knew him only as *Tuck*. About twenty years older, Tuck was one of the infamous rocket scientists with NASA before the moon missions ceased. He was also one of the least motivated telecom engineers since he considered his current job insignificant and boring compared to the long-gone space race excitement.

Everyone warned Dan that Tuck could charm him into doing his work. With an ever-present cigar clenched between his teeth, Tuck was a great communicator, a wonderful storyteller, and an expert persuader. He was always upbeat, animated, and interesting. Unfortunately, Graham was paired with one of the laziest men he had ever met. Nevertheless, when Tuck exercised his full skill set, his associates never even realized he had entrapped them under his spell. And yes, Dan fell under that influence and handled a lot of Tuck's responsibilities while Tucker tried to look busy.

Tuck would conveniently disappear every day, explaining that he was "going field checking," the common phrase used by engineers headed to their areas to collect field notes. Tuck had taken this to a new art form, however, because he never actually returned with field notes and rarely submitted an engineering job. Graham realized he was working for Tuck, but he did not know how to disentangle himself from Tucker's snares. On the other hand, Dan actually learned a number of managerial lessons from Tuck, some positive and some rather negative. At one point, Tucker manipulated Graham into sharing authorship credits on an article detailing how to analyze and resolve customer complaints. While Graham did most of the analysis and writing, Tuck understood how to promote the piece and got it published in an important industry journal. Their work drew corporate attention that, in turn, eventually led to some positive career moves.

One day after a particularly long series of daily absences with no work to show for it, Tuck revealed why he had often disappeared. "Squirrels!" he said. "I got three bleeping squirrels living in my attic." He was coming into work every day, doing some insignificant work, ensuring Dan was on top of their shared service order issues, and returning home to occupy a lawn chair below the eaves of his house. Armed with a BB gun, Tuck camped out day after day attempting to catch a glimpse and take shots at the rodents as they exited a small hole near the roof. He never succeeded and gave up after several weeks.

After observing that Graham handled most of Tuck's service problems, Voorhees transferred Tucker to another district, where he eventually sought early retirement to avoid actual work. When Tuck left, Graham's fellow engineers quizzed him on why one would waste his time working with the well-known slacker. Dan thought long and hard about an appropriate response and finally knew precisely how to characterize Tuck. Dan explained, "Tuck was probably the greatest leader I have met in the company. He always knew exactly how to get everyone to work for him even though he had no formal authority! Every leader should be that good."

3

"I Want This Fixed!"

Like most employees, Dan Graham disliked working for abrasive, bullying managers. Somehow, though, he seemed to inherit a few over the years. Dan's immediate supervisor, Ron Whitman, was an outstanding leader but their division manager, Burt Larkin, was a notoriously demanding tyrant. He was so abrasive that his operating division (about 1,000 employees) held the dubious distinction of placing dead last in their company's employee satisfaction index. But more about that later.

Mr. Larkin enjoyed setting unrealistic goals and changing the objectives as a manager started to achieve them. He insisted on microtracking monthly results for multiple objectives in his operations department. In a pre-Excel world, his districts employed some two hundred two-foot by three-foot posters, stencils, and graphic chart tape to plot the results for their departments. When Larkin took over as division manager, he forced his districts to reassign several administrative assistants to full-time positions simply collecting, recording, and plotting results on the graphs. Along with several other districts in Larkin's division, each month they hurriedly finished the last poster, gathered the other 199 charts, and transported the unwieldy assemblage to the division conference room some twenty-five miles away. Secretly, the managers called it their monthly appearance "before the throne."

Larkin held these meetings from 7 a.m. to 7 p.m. or later. Each district manager and his or her supervising managers stood at the front of the conference room and presented the results on thirty or forty charts. Each time the graph dipped below the objective line for the month under review, Larkin badgered the presenting manager and peppered him or her with multiple questions. "That's unacceptable. When will you be in compliance? That's not good enough. I *want this fixed* before our next meeting!"

He also delighted in checking the previous month's commitments, accusing the presenter with his standard "You already used that excuse last month!" Frankly, it seemed as though he derived some sadistic pleasure while harassing his managers. To be sure, tracking results and comparing them to objectives is a fundamental management technique and essential in helping organizations focus on the goals important to their success. Today's more enlightened executives employ similar management-by-objective (MBO) meetings to identify problems and then coach, partner with, or empower their management teams to achieve improvements. Larkin, in contrast, used the process to identify the weakest managers, first for humiliation and then elimination. Over the several years that Dan attended them, Larkin succeeded in forcing several early retirements, three twelve-step relapses, and at least two heart attacks. In fact, Dan had been promoted to his position when his predecessor suffered one of those heart attacks a few months earlier. As was one of the younger members of the team, Graham was determined to avoid a similar fate.

On the wall behind his desk, a huge, beautifully framed painting of a water buffalo stared menacingly at all visitors to Larkin's office. The symbolism was not lost on anyone who entered. Larkin was the fittest in the herd and intent on surviving at all costs, fighting to the death if you crossed his path. Granted, water buffaloes are not predators thinning the herd by digesting their rivals, but the meanest and fittest retain their status by eliminating weaker adversaries. Either way, water buffaloes thin the herd, and Larkin embraced his mystical spirit animal in doing so! In a survival of the fittest tactic, these monthly meetings actually succeeded in identifying the weakest members of the management team. Carefully applying his traumatizing tactics, he eagerly awaited each month's meeting to select the one manager he would sacrifice. He delighted in watching his target fall behind, only to attract the hyenas and buzzards as the herd left them in the dusty distance.

Graham supervised the support group functions for his district. These included staff tasks that supported the field engineers and, specifically, project tracking and coordination. Drafting clerks, budget personnel, project coordinators, and construction scheduling all came under his oversight. He also supervised the administrative staff responsible for preparing all those *results posters* Larkin focused on every month. As the youngest, most inexperienced support manager in the company, he also found himself leading one of the more inexperienced support teams in the division. His group's performance clearly reflected that immaturity. A peer that managed the district's field engineers delighted in shrieking, "Support group failure!" whenever an administrative obstacle appeared before his engineering team. It was a good-natured jab, but secretly, Graham feared that his group's poor performance would eventually lead to Larkin's crosshairs as the monthly candidate for deselection.

As suspected, Larkin's attempt to thin the herd happened during Dan's first couple of monthly meetings with him. At the first, Dan delivered a series of detailed schedules tracking the progress of construction projects his district engineered. In an attempt to conserve copier usage, Graham erred on the side of having too few sets of the forty-three-page document and distributed only ten copies to the fifteen attendees nervously awaiting the 7 a.m. start. Precisely, to the second, Larkin hurried into the room, glanced at the manual spreadsheet's first handwritten entry, and barked, "Why was project 3792 postponed for delayed material? Who is responsible for missing the order date?" Then, before anyone could answer, he realized that several of the fifteen attendees were sharing their schedules. He hastily changed his query and demanded, with staccato delivery, "Who is responsible for failing to have enough copies?"

Now expecting that Larkin would bellow some form of audible disgust for an errant district objective, Dan had already rehearsed several possible responses. He knew that a quick, confident response might just help avoid that weakest animal label. However, all his practiced replies seemed inappropriate for the question on the table. He had not prepared an excuse for the lack of copies.

"I am, sir, but it will never happen again," Graham quickly (if not confidently) responded.

"See that it doesn't! *I want this fixed* before our next meeting!" Then, without pausing, Larkin revisited his first question. "Well, who missed the due date? I'm waiting!"

The remainder of that meeting was uneventful. As usual, it continued until noon when Larkin's executive secretary entered the conference room with exactly fifteen sub sandwiches of unknown variety and fifteen randomly selected soft drinks. Larkin would stop everything and glare at anyone disrupting the meeting as they rummaged through the sandwiches, so attendees learned to grab whichever was closest as the tray circled the table. They hurriedly consumed the lunch offerings and spent the rest of the day with indigestion. Upon returning to their engineering office in the late afternoon, a dozen associates lined the hallways to observe which members of the herd had fallen prey.

After that first meeting, Dan promised himself that he would supply all the copies Larkin could ever want—and then some—for the next meeting. He was not about to invite more embarrassment for failing to handle a simple task like delivering document copies. Larkin was intent on thinning the herd, but Dan was determined to survive his onslaught. If he was planning to single him out again, Dan was insistent it should be for some important failure in discharging real engineering responsibilities—not for underestimating the number of copies needed.

Thus, the following month, Graham was well prepared. He knew the gathering could grow to twenty-five or more so he ordered thirty sets. The bill for the printing service was over $400, but Dan viewed it as a direct investment in job security.

As the meeting got underway, Larkin opened his seventy-page document, intending to read line by line while demanding answers for any scheduling issue he observed. Instead, he paused, glanced around the room, and realized it was one of the smaller meetings of the year. He then eyed the pile of unused documents stacked in the center of the conference table. Dan was secretly pleased, expecting a pat on the back for having plenty of copies this time, even if they were not all needed. Then he heard, "Who is responsible for all these extra copies?" From the tone of his voice, it was clear that he was not at all pleased.

"I am, sir," a reluctant Graham announced, at once realizing that no one could ever win with this man.

Larkin tilted his head down and peered through his enormous eyeglasses. Dan saw that the lenses made his eyes appear two or three times larger than a normal human. Graham had seen this posturing before, but this stressful moment seemed to exaggerate the effect so that he finally realized exactly what he was seeing. Those were the enormous menacing eyes of a full-grown water buffalo! Glaring directly at Graham, Larkin said sarcastically, "What now? Do you have the *Xerox* concession too?"

"No, sir. It will never happen again." Dan almost uttered the phrase in its entirety before Larkin commenced growling.

"See that it doesn't! *I want this fixed* before our next meeting!"

Despite this exchange, the attendees all thought they had learned something at that very moment. Dan had just reached safe haven for the remainder of the meeting. It became clear that each person had to endure Larkin's wrath at least once during every meeting. They found that if a manager could arrange to get it out of the way quickly—for some trivial error—Larkin allowed them to escape the deselection process. They could avoid elimination and "remain in the herd" to survive another day.

Meetings went on that way for another year or so, each manager purposely adding some insignificant error to highlight at the beginning of their presentation. They all practiced saying, "Here's where we are, here's where we want to be, and here's how we're going to get there," as they slapped a three-foot pointer onto their preselected minor failure on a beautifully prepared poster. This permitted Larkin to paw the ground, snort, stomp, and charge. The managers knew that after this show of force on a nonfiring offense, they reached their sanctuary for the day. Any true problems that might appear later in their charts slipped by without so much as a head bob.

Not long after that, the company decided to work on its image and implemented an employee satisfaction survey. Rumor had it that the headquarters human resources department had received so many complaints about Larkin they had to act. The survey was anonymous but contained detailed questions about district and division activities. There were also several comment areas to add further incriminating detail. Everyone felt it their solemn duty to report on all the abuse they had suffered over the years, pointing to the tears, those who nearly collapsed from the stress, and the two who had suffered chest pains and hospital visits.

On a Monday morning six weeks later, Larkin received a hard copy of the report. The cover letter indicated that his division earned the worst results of all operating divisions in the company. Larkin wrote a personal note and attached it to the report. He had his secretary make one copy each for his three districts, and these arrived by courier that afternoon. The report found its way to Dan's office about 3 p.m. Larkin's handwritten note said, simply, "I want this fixed before our next meeting!" The next meeting was Friday! Yes, he instructed Dan to correct a massive employee satisfaction problem—the worst in the company—in four days. It so perfectly captured Larkin's style that it surprised no one. They could not help but find the humor in his absurd decree.

But the story did not end there. Company executives decided to reassign Larkin to—of all places—corporate headquarters in charge of *human resources for the company!* All his former employees found it preposterous and made jokes about the move. Some of them even asked, "How could upper management install a *non*human to lead the *human* resources department?"

Most managers failed to understand the wisdom behind the move, however. The reasoning became more apparent after a few months. That's when everyone began to hear rumors that Larkin was not performing well under all the direct scrutiny at the top. He was not meeting goals or expectations in his new job. More important, the executives saw Larkin's toxic tactics and inappropriate behaviors up close for a change. Just a few months after the move, Larkin announced his early retirement. He became the weakest link left behind for the hyenas. Upon hearing the news, everyone just hoped that at some point his new boss had yelled at him, "I want this fixed before our next meeting!"

4

Babbling PUCs, Beepers, and Stickmen

"Is this net tech support?" the voice on the phone asked.

"Yes, what's up?" Graham answered.

"This is Mike in toll at Ojus 4E. I think we have a babbling PUC here. Stuck bit or something. We're also getting slippage on about two hundred interoffice trunks. I referred those to a Mr. Heron several months ago before the split. He was supposed to have your local workers option for loop timing, but I never heard anything."

"Mr. Heron passed away last month. I'm handling his duties, so let me check into this and I'll get back with you later today." It was Dan's first week on the new tech support job and he was listening to what seemed like a foreign language.

The first day after the breakup of the Bell System under the Justice Department's divestiture guidelines, Dan Graham reported to Sam Rendell in his new regional network technical support (NTS) job. Although he had a significant amount of training for his earlier job under Whitman on the area transmission staff (ATS), Graham had very little expertise for this NTS position. The ATS job had focused on local customers with predigital analog equipment problems. His new NTS staff, on the other hand, concentrated on interstate fiber optic systems serving 100,000 customers or more. Graham was overwhelmed, and he was beginning to think he had made a serious error in agreeing to the transfer.

Dan was responsible for supporting some 250 regional telecom equipment buildings. These multifloor offices had hundreds of rows of eleven-foot-high equipment bays filled with switching equipment, long-distance transmission systems, optical fiber apparatus, and other such objects. The workers in these offices were experts on repairing many of the standard systems but rarely had time to search for information on more obscure issues. That's where Dan's team entered the picture. At that point, however, Graham was often as clueless as the workers calling for assistance. Fortunately, he was good at researching and locating information, and he had lots of BSPs.

In the days before Google and the internet, almost every district office in old AT&T had one room set aside for its Bell System Practices (BSP) library. They covered nearly all the information a regional operating company needed to function in the telecommunications industry. They held thousands of fifty- to five-hundred-page write-ups all indexed precisely in the so-called nine-digit series. A worker could locate accounting information, safety rules, local cable installation details, complex equipment maintenance, and so forth. Most offices had standing orders to receive updates in the mail daily and administrative assistants in larger offices had full-time jobs removing outdated BSPs from the black, four-inch binders and replacing them with the updates. Smaller offices often had no time to file the updates and simply stacked them in piles three or four feet high around the office. In Dan's NTS office, the BSP library was the largest he had ever seen and essential to their operation. A full-time admin assistant served as the BSP "librarian" in a twenty-foot by twenty-foot room ringed with floor-to-ceiling shelves. The neatly filed practices covered everything a worker needed for installing and repairing nearly every piece of equipment the company owned, and some of that dated to the early 1900s.

After receiving Mike's call, Graham started to decode the words he heard. Fortunately, he could access information on any given trouble by just entering that library, and it was just thirty steps from his desk. Dan already understood that the word *toll* was a reference to the interoffice trunks that connected the office to distant cities. His next clue was the phrase *Ojus 4E*. Ojus, he knew, was the small town where a huge, four-story switching machine was located. It handled long-distance telephone traffic in and out of Miami. The number and letter were Mike's abbreviation for AT&T's office designation: a *Number 4 Electronic Switching System*, essentially a massive computer that could connect any Miami customer to any other telephone on earth. Graham headed to the BSP room to look for switching and transmission equipment common to the 4ESS machines to find a reference to *PUCs* or *stuck bits*. He soon found info describing a so-called Peripheral Unit Controller, a small computer system that controls some of the digital transmission equipment. He browsed through the 140-page practice and found a reference to a unique condition called *babble* that sometimes afflicted the PUC. He also found information on a malfunction caused by an error commonly called a *stuck bit*. That was an anomaly like an unidentified glitch causing a PC to freeze and then requiring a restart. It turned out that a babbling PUC and/or a stuck bit was likely indicative of a defective unit similar to a faltering hard drive that corrupts PC data files. Dan found a couple of BSP pages showing how to replace the plug-in and faxed them to the office for a relatively simple repair.

Next, he began looking into the *slippage* and *loop timing* issues. He found a BSP explaining these terms in relation to connecting two or more digital systems. Each office's computer had its own digital clock that established how signals were decoded. If the first clock was running a nanosecond differently from the second one, they introduced data errors. For voice conversations, it produced loud, annoying clicks every second as the data streams "slipped" while trying to synchronize with their remote equipment. If the channels were carrying important data, the error rates would cause the entire network to fail. And if that network was serving a series of banks? Well, that just wasn't acceptable!

Graham found a Task Oriented Practice (TOPS) document in one of the BSP binders and was surprised to learn that it offered step-by-step instructions to resolve digital slippage concerns. Quickly thumbing through the pages, he soon located a couple of helpful notes near the end of the 199-page document. Within exactly seven minutes of entering the library, he found the precise explanation Mike needed to adjust the controls and correct the slippage problem. He sent the information out to Mike by fax but knew that he would probably have to supervise the task across several other offices exhibiting the same effects. Later that afternoon, Mike called back to report on his progress.

"Hey Danny, I got the PUC replaced and started changing the loop timing options. Everything looks good. Thanks. You guys really are experts on this stuff. I'm glad we have you. By the way, don't mention this to my boss; she thinks we figured it out on our own."

"Well, that's why we're here," Graham explained. "Call back anytime."

Dan had intended to deflect the praise but stopped short. He wanted to explain that the only difference between himself and Mike was that he (Dan) had a better library and an extra seven minutes to find the answers. Instead, he left Mike with the impression that he was truly a technical "wizard." With episodes like this, Dan began to gain a reputation as an expert in the digital transmission field, and that tended to increase his personal influence in the region. He was seeing firsthand that information and knowledge was truly *power* in a world ruled by technology.

When Dan's regional staff initially formed shortly before divestiture, its stated mission was supporting the operations workers in the switching offices throughout the region. The Corporate Maintenance Engineers, an even higher tier of support, had handled some of these duties during the transition but they could not keep pace with the workload. Moreover, they never showed the local workers how to solve a trouble. Instead, they stealthily entered, set up a pile of test equipment and instruments, worked by themselves for a day or two, and simply advised the office supervisor that "everything was fixed" as they left. None of the workers learned anything from the process and, therefore, remained just as inefficient when faced with a similar issue in the future. Dan's company established the NTS groups to resolve these inefficiencies by recruiting *operations* people rather than *engineering* personnel to mirror the functions of their frontline workers more closely. The elite of the elite maintenance engineers still stepped in for the more complex issues, but they funneled their daily support tasks to Dan and the NTS folks instead.

Not long after Graham worked with Mike in Ojus, he made the mistake of inviting an old Maintenance Engineering friend to accompany him to a couple of the offices to train the local workforce. He wanted to instruct them on how to make the loop-timing settings so they could handle the other two hundred systems. Vik Borgenhoff agreed, and they met at one of the suspect locations. Dan helped Vik haul in multiple test instruments and troubleshooting equipment, all the while wondering why Borgenhoff needed it just to show the workers how to throw a simple switch. Finding the right circuit pack in a sea of similar units was the hard part. Inspecting and adjusting a single microswitch was the easy part. It required no careful examination, no fancy test gear, and no long-term studies. They finally located the right row, correct bay, specific relay rack, and proper channel bank shelf among thousands of other gray panels. Then Vik set up all his test equipment and pulled out an entire set of schematic diagrams showing the inner circuitry of each unit along with the wiring diagrams for the entire bay of equipment. These were documents rarely seen by the average worker and typically only accessed by maintenance engineers. Telephone equipment manufacturers designed their gear for plug-and-play operation so, like changing a lightbulb or a fuse in an auto, a tech did not need to understand the inner workings just to make a quick fix.

Graham challenged Borgenhoff, asking, "What's up? Do you think we'll have a problem after we set the option?"

"No," Vik replied, annoyed that he had to explain. "We just need to start at the beginning to make absolutely sure of the trouble before we start monkeying around with all the settings."

"Wait a minute," Dan cautioned. "We're here to show these guys how to quickly locate and reset the timing options. You're talking about an eight-hour analysis for no reason."

"Look, you asked me to come out here with you. This is how I work. I don't believe in a bunch of haphazard quick fixes. When I'm finished, I'll know for sure that we only need to change that one option." Borgenhoff's condescending tone spoke volumes.

Dan yielded to Vik's expertise for about an hour before he could no longer wait. He reached up to the Optical Interface Unit and easily threw the tiny option switch. Vik's equipment immediately stabilized, showing the system operating properly. Borgenhoff protested excitedly, "What are you doing? You're screwing up everything!"

Graham started to argue but suddenly detected the larger truth in Vik's statement. Borgenhoff was sensing the threat that Dan's new support function posed rather than the issue they were reviewing that moment. Vik had built a career on handling his duties exactly this way. He knew beyond any doubt how to resolve a hundred different troubles just by walking into an office and flipping a switch here or there. However, he knew that if he did not put on a spectacular show like some modern-day shaman with all the magical test gear, complicated schematics, and extended testing, the workers would realize that anyone could easily handle 80 percent of the job. Then Vik and his colleagues would lose their mystique as the workers pulled back the curtain to reveal ordinary men whose services were now obsolete.

While he was surprised at how Vik, a senior management employee, could behave like this, Dan had observed it before with their nonmanagement workers. That began when Rendell asked Graham to conduct a "riding exercise" with a cable repair crew to review their approach to repairing trunk cable defects. Since each pair of wires in the interoffice cables supported a dozen digital channels, a single defect resulted in a twelve-to-one loss in telephone traffic. Being new in the area, no one suspected that

Dan was going "undercover" to review the crew's methods. Introduced as a prospective crew member, they allowed him to accompany them to see what he might be doing in the future. Their supervisor had given this crew of five a weeklong job to find several defective copper wires in three miles of cable, repair them, and then install new digital equipment for long-distance service. During the week, Dan accompanied crew members as they stopped for midmorning breakfasts, enjoyed three-hour lunch breaks, and picked up home pool supplies. They also planned painfully slow, plodding troubleshooting methods so their boss would not reassign them to a new task before the end of the week. Since they had to pump water out of their underground maintenance holes for over an hour every day before entering, they also made sure to stop working just in time each day so that they had to reopen the same hole the next morning, wasting another hour of prep time.

Having promised they would analyze and complete the repairs before close of business on Friday, they finally opened a remote utility access hole on Thursday afternoon after an extended lunch. They pumped it, prepped it, and went directly to the correct splice case. They opened the splice, repaired four wires, and buttoned it up, all within thirty minutes. The crew refused to take an extra fifteen minutes to repair another twelve wires while the splice remained open. They explained that they knew this splice always had faulty wires. They opened it about once a month, after a long troubleshooting process, to fix the two or three wires needed to meet a due date. Dan finally realized that all the testing from Monday morning was simply a sham. The crew also explained they never repaired the extra wires because that guaranteed enough work for about three or four more weeklong episodes. Reviewing all that had happened in the last week, Dan realized that a crew of five expended over 150 hours across four days on a job that two cable repair crew members could have completed on Monday morning before lunch. All to safeguard their future job security.

Dan made sure never to visit that area again. He had outworn his welcome after reporting his findings to the district manager.

Owing to some of this insight and success, Rendell asked him to take over supervision of a small team of NTS managers in their district. Other members of the one-hundred-manager NTS district had affectionately labeled these three first levels "the stickmen." Jon, Rob, and JW were elite experts in just about every aspect of the telecom equipment world. They were under constant stress while handling numerous calls every day, rarely ate lunch, and smoked constantly. Graham suspected that those conditions explained why each man was six feet tall and painfully thin. Rob was so thin that he purchased his trousers in the boys sections to find small enough waist sizes. Consequently, his inseams were always four inches too short. Despite their emaciated appearance, the entire district knew that you could not solve certain problems without their input. It was common to hear one of the other supervisors in an important meeting saying, "Hey, go get the stickmen and see what they say about this."

The stickmen reported to Arnie Wagner, a senior engineering manager half a step below a full second-level supervisor, a reporting structure common on the staff. Arnie was a transplant from the New York telephone company where he had supervised a crew serving one-square block of Manhattan skyscraper businesses. While there, supervisors in the business districts wore expensive suits, ties, and fedoras to present a professional image while dealing with their corporate clients. He often reminded Graham that one of the proudest days of his life was when he "got the hat," a phrase the Manhattan telecommunications workers applied to a promotion from nonmanagement to management. After transferring to the tourist state as a middle-aged telephone man, he put on quite a bit of weight so that, at five feet, five inches tall, he was decidedly plump. Referring to his round shape, some of the staff managers teased him and his stickmen, calling them the *digital* crew "three ones and a zero."

Arnie insisted on taking Graham and a couple of other managers to a deli within walking distance a couple of times a week for a quick break. With a thick New York accent and a lack of patience, Wagner would sit and snap his fingers for the wait staff. He then delivered his very precise order.

"Hi, dear. I'll have my usual: *gahlick* bagel, *boint.* Not toasted, *boint!* I'll send it back if it ain't *boint, unnastan?* And *buttah* it. Oh, and a cup of coffee, black. Thank you, dear."

When the food arrived, Arnie tore one side of the singed bagel in half and proceeded to dip the blackened, buttered, garlicky concoction into the coffee before eating it. Then, while chewing with his mouth half-opened, he would describe an issue his stickmen had handled the previous day.

"So what do you think we should do in a case like that?" he would query each in turn, preparing for a confrontation with his three employees. Returning from his morning break and smelling of garlic, Arnie would hold a brief meeting with his stickmen. It usually started with "Guys, put 'em on hold and *get* in the room *now!"* referring to the small conference room near their cubicles. The door would then slam, and Arnie's yelling would only occasionally exceed the decibel threshold necessary to escape the soundproofed door. Bellowing about how they handled one of their trouble calls from the previous day, he would then explain how they should have handled it—based precisely on the advice he just received while digesting his overcooked bagel.

Despite his eccentricities and confrontational management style, Graham learned a great deal while observing the solid customer focus Wagner had refined in Manhattan. One memorable lesson was simply learning to listen. After one of Arnie's infamous "conferences" with the stickmen, he entered Dan's office and announced he had a couple of important issues he needed to discuss. At the time, Graham was practicing his *open-door* policy to encourage his new employees to communicate anytime they felt the need. Unfortunately, Dan was usually not fully engaged in the process. Believing he was a good multitasker, Dan always invited one of the workers to sit but continued to handle email or in-basket duties. He also interrupted any conversation—no matter how important—to take a random phone call.

When he asked Arnie to sit, he quickly said, "OK, what's up?" and then turned his back to Wagner as he continued reviewing and responding to email. After a minute or two, he realized he had heard nothing from Wagner. Turning around, he observed Arnie sitting patiently while just staring at him. Graham repeated his greeting and again asked, "So what did you want?"

"Look, don't turn away. I came in here to talk, and I need your attention. I'll understand if you're too busy. Just tell me and I'll come back later. Otherwise, I need to talk, and I need you to actually listen."

Wagner came across as polite and sincere, and the message hit Dan hard. He felt his face blushing with embarrassment as he grasped, for the first time in his career, the rude behavior he had practiced for years. After thinking for a moment, he said, "Arnie, you're right. That's a lesson I needed. Let's start again."

Wagner wanted to discuss a possible solution to the poor reputation he had developed prior to Dan's arrival. Some of the staff managers complained that Arnie seemed to disappear every few days for several hours, explaining only that he was "checking on some customers." Dan was aware of the reputation and Rendell even mentioned it when they discussed the new supervisory assignment. Rendell suspected that Wagner was eyeing retirement and suggested that Dan figure out how to pin him down a little better or encourage him to move on. Sitting in front of Dan, Wagner broached the subject first and said, "Look, I'm gonna put in my papers soon and I've been handling some personal business for the past six months to get ready. I don't want everyone knowing my business so I haven't talked about it. I kept telling Mr. Rendell that I'd be happy to carry a pager like I did in Manhattan but couldn't get any buy-in. He thinks that would give me official approval to wander anywhere without restrictions. That's just not the right way to look at it."

Graham began to see an opportunity to handle the situation.

Cell phones were yet to be introduced in the mid-1980s, so *beepers* or *pagers* were often used to contact workers who were "out in the field." The inability to track Arnie sounded suspiciously like the Tuck Tucker dilemma Dan observed a decade earlier. Now, however, the new beepers allowed a supervisor to enter a phone number for the employee to call. Graham decided to use the "wireless leash" to tether Wagner until he formally retired. They agreed that Arnie would requisition a pager; he would keep it with him whenever he left the office, he would return any call to any number sent to him, and he would make sure to do so within fifteen minutes of any page. Graham then told him to share his pager number with the support supervisors on staff and all the field supervisors throughout the state. Graham also handed him a handful of quarters and told him to make sure he always carried a pocketful to use in the nearest public payphone. (Yes, they existed before cell phones too.)

At first, the other supervisors and Rendell felt Graham was just shirking his responsibilities by not laying down the law. Dan met with them and explained, "No one here handled Arnie before I got here. Trust me to handle it my way for a while. If it doesn't work out, I'll try it your way. By the way, I expect you to test it out and let me know anytime you could not get in touch with him." Graham then warned Wagner that the managers planned to test the plan and would report back anytime Wagner was unreachable.

"Bring 'em on. Believe me on this. I won't let you down," Arnie bragged.

The plan worked brilliantly. For the first time in over a year, anyone could reach Arnie anytime, anywhere. Dan did not care exactly where he was every couple of days, so long as Wagner provided whatever assistance the caller needed or relayed the questions to his stickmen on a subsequent call. After a few weeks of testing Wagner's availability, the constant contacts subsided and the system then cooked along nicely for several months until, one afternoon, Arnie walked into Dan's office and said, "Thanks again for trusting me. I got all my concerns worked out with everybody now. Here are my retirement papers. It's official in two weeks."

When Arnie left, Dan took over direct supervision of the stickmen. While they would occasionally visit an office to train personnel, they typically just handled individual phone calls and directed the worker while he or she remained on the call. They then hung up, smoked, drank one of a dozen cups of coffee each day, and waited a minute or two for the next call. The employee on that next call was likely requesting information on exactly the same issue they had just handled for another office.

After Graham observed this behavior for several weeks, he began making notes on the types of calls the stickmen were receiving. He had wanted Wagner to handle some of these duties before he left but realized he was only interested in his imminent retirement. Instead, Dan started categorizing the issues and found he could usually associate them with eight or nine common causes. Occasionally they had to research something completely different, but most of the requests fell neatly into the expected categories. Graham then tried to apply the "Pareto Principle" he learned in the Total Quality Management classes the company offered. Typically called the 80/20 rule, it boiled down to a rather simple and commonsense fact: 80 percent of a system's troubles typically result from only 20 percent of the possible causes. Applying it to the stickmen, he proposed they could eliminate about 80 percent of their workload by simply producing job aid cards that explained how to handle the most common daily problems. As they looked through the top categories, they realized that even addressing a couple of them, the so-called "low-hanging fruit," could eliminate over half of their daily workload when thoroughly implemented.

Graham asked his team to begin designing three-inch by seven-inch laminated cards to fit in a shirt pocket. Each color-coded card outlined a systematic investigation, troubleshooting method, or any other detail to assist the technician. The card also provided numbers to the support group in case they had more questions. After several months of prep work, Graham distributed a stack of them to every office. When a tech called with one of the standard questions after that, a stickman would simply say, "Go grab the green card we sent you, and follow the instructions. If you have any difficulty, call me back immediately." After about six months, their workload had dwindled to the point they were beginning to worry about keeping their jobs. Before they could become too concerned, however, Dan received the call about the breakup of their district.

5

A Broom, a Pumpkin, and a Bunny

Bill Jones summoned Dan to a meeting regarding a reorganization project that would combine several former districts into a five-hundred-worker operations center. Dan was told he would be supervising some of the managers and work groups in that division. Called the Circuit Provisioning Center (CPC), most of its workers prepared and emailed information (called Work Order Record Details or WORD documents) to some 250 central telephone offices in their region. The documents provided detailed instructions for office technicians to install and connect equipment for circuits that extended for hundreds of miles through multiple telecom offices. Dan was pleased to learn that at least he and his stickmen would be working with many of the same office supervisors and technicians they had been supporting while serving in their net tech support function.

The WORD documents, prepared by about 80 percent of the CPC workforce, instructed office technicians how to install voice or digital data circuits, fiber optic systems, or other sophisticated telecom equipment. The remaining 20 percent of the CPC workers provided support to those same field workers during installations or repairs. Bill explained that Dan would supervise the new group, made up of several combined functions and totaling about one hundred workers with ten managers. When his new Design Assistance Bureau (DAB) received a call from anywhere in the southeastern US, his team would provide the outside workforce with expert advice while installing or restoring service. Other groups under his direction issued information for area code changes, interoffice trunks, or special circuits requested by the FAA, FBI, or FCC. The new group also included a small quality control function that oversaw all efforts of the remaining four hundred circuit designers.

Jones explained, "We have a lot of computerized automation going on. I expect the five hundred workers in this department to dwindle down to about two hundred over the next few years as their manual work functions are replaced with software programs. I also expect you to work yourself out of a job during that time. I'm retiring soon so you'll have to handle all the HR and union issues as you displace our workers. By the way, you probably ought to watch out for Gloria Helmsley. She's one of the techs in your DAB group and the vice president of the union here. She is a true leader among her constituents and will have *you* working for her, too, if you're not real careful."

As their jobs in Rendell's district were phased out, Graham prepared the paperwork to bring the stickmen with him to the new district. Their job would evolve from handling equipment problems to handling individual customer circuit troubles instead. Dan thought they could complement the DAB group as a second-tier support function focusing on the problems too complex for the DAB's nonmanagement workers. Lou, the DAB supervisor, was openly fearful of the merger as he felt Graham would eliminate his job when the more experienced stickmen arrived. This concern festered as the two groups faced several months of delay before the merger. One of the stickmen, JW, all but threatened the new group with "You just wait 'til Mr. Graham takes over. We'll get you people in line!"

Recognizing the looming tension, Dan needed a quick method to smooth over the hard feelings. Working closely with Graham for the previous three years, Jon, Rob, and JW believed Dan would direct them to devise the new workflows that would likely seal Lou's fate. They were surprised when Graham asked Lou to develop the new organizational structure and propose the new workflows. It broke the tension and put Lou and the DAB personnel more at ease. Lou immediately placed himself in the same category as the NTS support managers to troubleshoot second-tier problems his DAB personnel could not quickly resolve. Although the stickmen did not like the arrangement, Graham explained that they had worked together for a long time, and he trusted they could handle any rearranged workflows Lou threw at them. Realizing Dan was privately complimenting their abilities, the stickmen accepted Lou's proposal and the groups merged with few conflicts. Short of issuing a decree, Dan had never devised a contingency plan to resolve the inefficient system Lou proposed. Fortunately, Lou soon realized he did not possess the necessary background and requested a return to his area of expertise, simply supervising his DAB personnel. Dan was relieved and agreed. He knew that empowering an employee to come to the right conclusion was dangerous. While it made Dan look like a master of situational leadership theory, he privately knew that he was just lucky that it all worked out as well as it did.

When he finally felt the situation was under control, the union VP, Gloria Helmsley, introduced herself in a very memorable way. She wanted to outline her expectations for cooperation on a list of issues needing their "joint" attention in the future. Gloria sat just twenty feet from Dan's office in a small cubicle where she handled standard DAB tasks all day long. She was also frequently "off duty" handling official union activities. Gloria was at least ten years older than Dan and spoke with a deep, gravelly voice finely crafted from thirty-five years of smoking. On the day she entered Graham's office with her talking points, she was dressed as a large, orange pumpkin with only her head, forearms, and legs (below the knees) visible.

"Mr. Graham, we've spoken a couple times since you've been here over the last few weeks, but I think it's time we discuss a few things," the woman in the pumpkin suit said. It was the day before Halloween and the CPC had always participated in the twelve-story building's annual costume contest. Several hundred CPC employees competed with eleven other floors of workers from marketing, accounting, and customer service, all dressed to win recognition for their department. The union and one of the telecom's national service clubs teamed to sponsor the event as a way of building teamwork and raising money for local charities. Gloria, of course, was one of the primary directors of the events.

Having worked with union employees for years, Dan knew that only the union contract's formal grievance process required him to meet on official union problems. However, he always believed an open dialogue was a good idea if both parties conducted themselves in a respectful manner. To be sure, grievances were typically a response to disciplinary action taken by management. Supervisors knew that the concept of *discipline,* as spelled out in the working agreement, was not *punishment.* Instead, the four steps aimed to "rehabilitate" an employee who had strayed from satisfactory performance. Bosses facing a union steward representing a grieving employee often quoted the usual cliché "All we want is *a fair day's work for a fair day's pay.*"

"Agreed, but these four steps, *counsel, warn, suspend, and fire,* can lead to termination of one of my members and we just won't permit that," a diligent steward would always counter. It was a well-known ritual that played out hundreds of times annually across the corporation. Both sides knew exactly what to expect, exactly what to say, and exactly how to settle the disagreement. Dan always thought of it as a kind of choreographed dance. Once you learned the moves as a new manager, you could always rely on your dance partner to execute the steps without stepping on your toes!

With all this in mind, Gloria knew that Dan could refuse her request, but he agreed anyway. So standing in front of his desk, Graham beheld the union's vice president in an orange costume nearly too wide to fit through the door. She remained standing because her pumpkin suit would not permit her to sit. She held a document with talking points but was unable to transfer it from one hand to the other as her arms only extended through the suit at the elbow. Having difficulty adjusting her reading glasses, Dan finally assisted her with that task. For two or three minutes, she attempted to read the discussion items from her list. After fighting with the document and her glasses, she finally said, "Let's do this later. This was not a good time." Secretly relieved, Dan agreed. He was having a difficult time maintaining his composure. It was all he could do to avoid laughing out loud as he watched the large, orange character turn and waddle out of his office.

When they next met, Gloria apologized for making a bad impression during the first official meeting but promised to make up for it. She then proceeded to cite, rapid fire, a number of issues about which her CPC union constituents complained. "I'll be working with you on these problems in the future, and I'm hoping we can avoid any messy grievance proceedings," she said politely but forcefully. Thus began several weeks of daily conferences with Gloria, usually starting with "Have you had a chance to do anything about …" after which she listed three or four items she had assigned to Dan for handling.

After a month, Jones dropped by to ask how things were going. "By the way, has Gloria got you working for her yet?" It suddenly occurred to Graham that yes, he was indeed working for Gloria.

Dan was slow to answer as he struggled to verbalize a satisfactory response. "Well, I'm working with her on a few issues, but I'm about to button that up."

"Thought so." Jones grinned and walked away while muttering to himself.

Graham finally realized he needed to develop a plan for a preemptive approach. Over the next couple of weeks, he decided to stand near her desk and greet her as she arrived every morning. He would then mention some trivial union-related item he wanted her to check into "to help improve relations with the members." This seemed to get the message across, and after a few weeks, an understood truce went into effect.

Thanks to some of Gloria's input, all the groups started working well together as intended. The DAB gradually became a mini call center handling all facets of technical support. DAB workers went into action when they found a so-called DAB ticket filed in their computer bin by one of 3,000 field workers. Alternatively, the field workforce would just call in with a problem and the phone system would direct it to the correct DAB employee. The DAB member would access the circuit or equipment information through the databases and then stay on the line while they jointly conducted tests to analyze the problem. The DAB worker would then update the records and close out the ticket. Finally, they charged the error to the person or group that created the problem. When the DAB folks failed to solve a problem, one of the stickmen would receive the handoff and proceed with more sophisticated troubleshooting.

The district's four hundred circuit designers generated many of the errors due to inaccuracies in the WORD documents they issued. Only a small percentage of documents exhibited errors, but the enormous service order volumes resulted in significant work content for the DAB every day. Since one of Lou's responsibilities involved quality control, he produced a monthly report assigning DAB ticket error rates to each of the twenty-five design groups. The design groups answered to three other second levels, Dan's peers, and fellow supervising engineers.

Dan had replaced Lou's former boss, Jonas Moran, when Bell Labs tapped Moran to head one of their engineering groups. Jonas was a technical wizard but was often confused by the mundane aspects of management. Lou's quality control function created a major problem for Moran because every first level, committed to maintaining minimal error percentages, challenged every monthly report. DAB members could charge errors to about ten cause codes including inventory errors, installation errors, equipment problems, or designer errors. Most of the codes were self-explanatory, but some were open to interpretation. When in doubt, Lou typically charged them internally to the district's circuit designers because most other codes implied errors outside his jurisdiction. The first-level supervisors, of course, retained the right to challenge each charge to reduce his or her error rate. Rather than taking steps to eliminate the monthly disputes, Moran encouraged the misbehavior by convening a monthly *Error Court* to hear both sides. Then, after a formal deliberation, Jonas would make a judicial ruling on each disagreement. With twenty-five supervisors, the proceedings could take several days. One supervisor, Bob Honeycutt, went out of his way to force the issue every month.

Realizing that Lou and Bob would soon approach him for their monthly hearing, Dan met with Bob's second-level supervisor, Sam, who explained he never approved of Moran's monthly court hearings. He simply wanted his first levels to accept the error reports at face value and address the systemic problems they could actually control. Instead, the supervisors enjoyed focusing on the loopholes and arguing the technicalities. Dan reassured him, "Let me handle it. I think we can put an end to the nonsense once and for all."

The day for the hearings finally arrived and Bob and Lou were up first in his office. Graham sat politely and listened to an hour of convoluted and boring explanations. Both sides finally rested their cases and turned to Graham for a ruling. Dan predicted that if he refused to encourage or reward their behavior, they would soon see that the meetings were unnecessary. Dan paused thoughtfully and finally said, "Bob, you understand that Lou reports to me. Therefore, from this point forward, I will agree with however Lou rules on all error codes in the future. That way, we can discontinue these meetings."

Bob was shocked at the response and mumbled something about being unfair. Lou, on the other hand, felt vindicated and appeared quite smug. While they both sat there, however, Graham told Bob that he knew exactly where Lou parked his car and that he would not be surprised if Lou had a flat tire when he left that afternoon. Then, in an effort to drive home the outrageous point, Dan explained, "An ice pick stuck in the sidewall works very nicely and it can't be repaired!"

Lou was suddenly dismayed at the decision. Graham simply wanted them to realize they had to work together and that they had to face consequences on the job when they chose to fight. He also wanted them to understand they could not relinquish their responsibilities to a supervisor to make their decisions for them every month as in the past. Dan turned back to Bob and said, "Now if you don't approve of how I'm handling this, I am offering a simple alternative. Just bring me the broomstick of the wicked witch of the west!"

Both supervisors were utterly confused and thought Graham had perhaps suffered a mental breakdown. "What the—what exactly does that mean?" Bob asked.

"Your boss told me he did not approve of his supervisors constantly arguing loopholes. He wants you solving problems," Dan replied. "So anytime you want Lou to reverse his decision, you bring me a note from Sam approving the change and I will immediately overrule Lou, no matter what it is."

Finally grasping the *Wizard of Oz* analogy and realizing that Graham was directing him to complete a nearly impossible task, Bob realized that procuring Sam's "broom" would not be so easy. Dan never had to meet with the two again "in court." Unfortunately, Honeycutt was not satisfied that easily and found other ways to complain.

Several weeks after the hearing, Honeycutt stormed into Graham's office and said, "I got a real problem with Coleman. He's agreed to some nearly impossible due dates. You've gotta do something with that marketing team!"

Reporting jointly to Dan and Beverly Dove from Marketing, Jack Coleman served as a CPC representative to the state marketing team that reviewed and approved large telecommunications projects for the region. If a bank wanted to connect one hundred branches with high-speed optical fiber service, for example, the team would review the design, installation, and due dates to confirm that the CPC and outside operations personnel could meet the commitments. Jack's job always required a compromise between marketing's desire to seal a deal with a rapid completion date while recognizing the operations department's need to reserve and schedule the necessary labor. Dan had several CPC members on the team stationed throughout the state while sharing supervisory duties in a *matrix* structure with Dove. A matrix arrangement required each team member to report to a supervisor from operations and one from marketing simultaneously to reach a compromise on every large project that would satisfy both departments. It also violated one of the fundamental rules of management: *unity of command.* Although the structure seemed to work well in certain global companies like Procter & Gamble, it was destined for failure in Dan's telecom. He and Dove had frequent disagreements over the performance of their assigned team members. Moreover, Jack hated reporting to the two supervisors, especially when Graham congratulated him for a good job setting realistic dates while Beverly chastised him for betraying the marketing folks and jeopardizing a big sale.

When Graham summoned Jack to his office, Coleman was sure he would face another scolding lecture session like those previously conducted by Jonas Moran to satisfy Beverly. This time, however, the operations people were angry with Jack and demanding the official reprimand. As Jack took his seat in front of Graham, he started nervously explaining why he had approved the project's shortened schedule and then waited for the stern rebuke. Graham said nothing; he just listened. He listened so long, in fact, that Jack became even more nervous, awaiting the fireworks. Graham said, finally, "How long have we been in here?"

Jack looked at his watch and reported, "Twenty-five minutes, I think."

"Good," Dan said. "I think that should just about do it. Anything else you want to talk about?"

"Ah, no. But what about ..." Jack responded nervously.

Dan explained that he understood the dilemma Jack faced every day in that awkward management structure and knew he would never please both parties.

"Jack, would it do any good to fuss and fume about your decisions? Would it change anything? Look, we may have to put on this little charade a few more times in the future to make everybody happy, but it'll only work if you react the right way when you leave." Dan then explained that, without lying, he should report to the curious that they did not *ever* want to endure one of those meetings. Graham had employed the same answer all those years earlier after working on the trunking project and emerging from Cy's office while still a junior engineer. It worked.

Not long after these incidents, Bill called Dan into his office and explained that he was finally retiring in about a month. He said, "By the way, I turned your name in for this executive expedition assessment program they're running. I guess they're trying to identify a few youngsters to move up in the company." He went on to explain that the company populated most of the sessions with up-and-coming strategic planners, the *unquestioned* best and brightest. However, they threw in a few older operations people like Dan just to round out each session. Their participation added a kind of experimental *control* group, establishing a baseline to observe how far the young superstars could outperform the "old operations slugs." Without explicitly stating it, Bill implied that thirty-nine-year-old Dan would attend as one of these *control* subjects.

The executive expedition firm had devised a series of activities to evaluate the leadership attributes of sixty or so second-level managers in the state. All the rage at the time in corporate America, these expeditions gathered about twenty managers per session, administered Myers-Briggs personality tests, flew them to a remote area, and observed their actions during a four-day scripted ordeal in the wilderness. Dan quickly affirmed his role in the experiment as he recognized only three or four other "nonpromotable" operations people in their late thirties and early forties.

All of the others were young, twentysomething planners. Dan knew several of the attendees and their reputations, so he was anticipating a lot of figurative scrambling like caged rodents trying to climb over each other to reach the cheese. Each of the *young Turks* entered with a strategy to impress the observers and win that prize: a clear path to a top executive position.

After flying to Atlanta, the groups traveled in two large vans for a couple of hours into the foothills. The observers said very little during the ride. As they approached a curve on a steep road, both vans pulled to the side and the drivers asked everyone to get out and stretch. As they exited, one observer handed a sheet of paper to a random participant, waved to the drivers, and both vans departed abruptly. The twenty managers stood in disbelief for several minutes, trying to discern what was happening. They began to realize this was part of the plan to see who might emerge as leaders. Recognizing he was just there to fill out a vacancy, Dan had determined to observe the egos as they fought for recognition. Three or four of the junior stars tore at the instruction sheet so they could take charge. Some ten years younger than Dan, the junior planners showed no interest in teamwork; they just wanted to lead the group into the adventure and on to glory.

After some fumbling, the team found its way to a forested area at the bottom of one of the foothills. Their map revealed they were near the Chattooga River and the rapids made famous during the filming of the early 1970s movie *Deliverance.*

The observers explained that the group would undertake an imaginary rescue mission to retrieve passengers from the supposed crash of a small plane. For the next three days, they rafted through the whitewater, slept in tents, and learned elementary mountain climbing rope knots and techniques. They were trained to assemble a complex array of ropes, pulleys, and stretchers into the so-called Tyrolean Rescue System. They were then going to employ the elaborate arrangement to ferry a live person (one of the observers) across a gorge. To turn up the anxiety, the observers warned them to learn their lessons well since a single rigging mistake could result in the stretcher (and observer) falling a hundred feet onto the boulders in the Chattooga.

At one point, Dan's junior boat "captain" gave so many mistaken commands while steering through the rapids that Graham popped out of their inflatable raft and hit the rocks. When they finally retrieved him, the other five passengers mutinied and put Dan in charge. Each step of the way, the junior leaders attempted to take charge and usually failed in some important aspect. When the observers were looking for teamwork, they saw people clawing for individual recognition. When they wanted to detect a focus on human relationships, they observed only task orientation. When looking for competent command, they saw incompetence.

The observers awakened the teams two or three times during the night and ordered them to relocate their camp or handle some other imaginary activity. With a series of countermanded orders and sleep deprivation, the observers intensified the tension and anxiety.

On the third day of the ordeal, one of Dan's older operations peers and a fellow experimental "control" member could take it no more. Tim Byner, a very quiet and unassuming manager who saw combat for several years as an army lieutenant in Vietnam, put a halt to the game. In an apparent wartime flashback episode, he started shouting orders at the entire group the evening before their final day's activities. The quiet person, invisible to that point, seemed suddenly inhabited by a forceful, commanding officer. He reassured the group that by following his lead they would complete their mission successfully. He even faced down the observers, threatening and *ordering* them to back off and stop inducing any more stress. They obeyed. In essence, Byner hijacked the entire leadership exercise, took over command, and scared everyone into submitting. The youngsters were particularly terrified, and most of them kept their distance. The intense look on his face alone was enough to frighten most of the group's members.

In any case, Tim was right about the mission's success. The observers reported that they were the only group of dozens from various companies to complete the task. Unfortunately, they also reported that Byner so corrupted the leadership exercise that it yielded nearly useless data for identifying future leaders. Not one of the junior planners on that expedition received a promotion; nor did Byner. He resumed his quiet, unassuming persona back on his regular job.

When Dan returned from the ordeal, he met the new district level leader transferred from the company's strategic planning department located at the opposite end of the state. Graham knew her from high school. Voted "most intelligent" in her senior year, Christie Dennard graduated as the salutatorian and promptly completed college with an engineering degree. The company hired her as a junior engineer the same year Dan started. Christie quickly ascended the corporate ladder and assumed a director's role in planning. After several years in that position, her sponsors transferred her to the CPC as a "grooming" opportunity. Since most key leaders required some experience in operations before the next promotion, the CPC seemed a good choice. The CPC, as part of the operations department, featured a mass of union workers she would confront daily rather than the elite group of highly educated but insulated managers she had previously supervised.

Clearly, Dennard was the most intelligent person Dan had ever worked for in the corporate world. Her kind of smarts served her well while leading the handpicked, gifted people populating the long-range planning groups. Naturally, Graham's experience in the operations world caused him some concern; he wondered how a leader from that highly professional, all-management environment would relate to five hundred union workers. The answer followed within the first few weeks. Dan was greatly disappointed to observe that his old high school friend's intelligence, the very same trait that translated so well in her strategic planning group, would *not* ensure her success in the *operations* world.

He also wondered how she would respond to him as her subordinate. In high school, Dennard was the girlfriend of Dan's best friend. They shared rides to school, attended football games together, and were in many of the same classes. He had not seen her in two decades and was clearly apprehensive about the situation. She soon addressed their new professional relationship in an unlikely manner. Early one morning, Christie called him to explain why she was late for work. "Graham, I have a flat tire. Just off the expressway near the exit ramp. I'm only a few miles from the building. I need to get it changed." Dan assumed she was waiting for her roadside service. She was not. "Well," she continued, "how long will it take you to get here?"

Crawling under the SUV ten minutes later, Graham lowered her spare tire from the undercarriage and replaced the flat. Oblivious, Christie never even mentioned the permanent grease stains on Dan's new, monogrammed dress shirt. A recent birthday gift from his wife, it was the first and last time he ever wore it.

Behind the scenes, Dennard began to count on Graham to offer advice on dealing with the new work groups. In public, she came across as constantly hurried, darting from one group to another and making impractical suggestions or throwing out harmless commands. She made a show of giving directions to Graham publicly in an attempt to suppress thoughts that, as an old friend, he would garner "most favored treatment." Their interaction approached ritual status with her regularly inventing some problem Graham's groups caused. Dan played along with the ruse, loudly assuring her, "We'll get right on it, boss!"

Over time, Christie attempted to learn more about Dan's groups but began to shy away from some of the more demanding aspects of the job. When Dan explained the so-called *escalation* process, Dennard quickly determined she did not want any part of it.

Escalations occurred when Lou's DAB group failed to resolve a trouble in a timely manner. The field tech's boss made a first-level escalation to

Lou, who then checked on the progress before a handoff to one of the stickmen. When they failed to fix it within a satisfactory period, the *second-level escalation* process started. Graham received that call from the field worker's supervisor. About 90 percent of the time when Dan's phone rang, he heard something like "Mr. Graham, this is Buzz in Orlando with a second-level escalation on Circuit ID CRQ5497." Dan knew it was an inefficient way of operating, but the company established the system to keep pushing a problem up the line so that all managers in the operations department understood the urgency. Most of the circuits they worked on were complex communication lines for such entities as banks, airports, and fire departments. The everyday circuits were important enough when they failed, but major circuits serving E911 centers or regional Air Traffic Control centers, for example, received the highest priority. They were also some of the more difficult circuits to troubleshoot and restore.

When Graham received one of these escalations, a regional FAA director would call him, saying, "Mr. Graham, this is Carol at Jacksonville Regional Air Traffic Control escalating a trouble on Circuit ID F279553. It has been down for thirty-seven minutes. JW on your staff has been working on it for twelve minutes. You are officially advised that if any air traffic is jeopardized due to this failure, you and your company will be held accountable." Within thirty minutes, Carol would place another call, this time to Dan's district level, Christie. Neither Dan nor Christie could make the repairs proceed any faster, but the escalation concept turned up the heat on any problem until someone, somewhere, somehow fixed the problem. Only one in 1,000 escalations got past the DAB, JW, and Graham. But with the volume they handled, that happened several times a week.

The first time Christie received a third-level escalation, she nearly panicked and sprinted up the stairs and down the hall to Graham's office. Slapping a note on his desk, she demanded, "What is going on here? Why am I getting this call? Who is handling this? What are you doing about it? Why is it still broken? When will—?"

"We are on it!" Graham interrupted and asked her to calm down and catch her breath. Perhaps she wasn't really panicked, but it sure seemed that way to Dan at that moment. "I already spoke to Carol in Jacksonville. She trusts us. She's fine. We've worked with her for years and always resolve her problems. She's just following official escalation policies and making a call every thirty minutes. I checked with JW a couple of minutes ago, and they are finishing up now. Everything is fine."

Dan was never comfortable with surprise escalations but had learned to cope with them. In fact, he hated surprises in any form. His wife never even planned surprise parties for his birthday, knowing that he would likely leave and not return for several hours when he heard a group of people yelling, "Surprise!" Early in his career, his supervisors recognized his poor reaction to last-minute changes too. A couple of his bosses purposely placed Graham in jobs that forced him to deal with them. All the trouble-handling positions he held had one thing in common: they involved one unexpected problem after another. Dan eventually realized that his supervisors were wise in selecting him for these jobs. They never intended to condition him to *accept* the surprises but predicted that he would discover how to *eliminate* them. Consequently, he always tried to invent procedures to help predict and prevent problems *before* they surprised him. He often told his subordinates that he did his best to refine and redefine the jobs of everyone surrounding him so that, ultimately, he could come to work every day with absolutely nothing to do. It was a lesson taught him by his old mentor, Tuck Tucker. Of course, Graham never achieved that state of bliss. As soon as he approached it, a boss would send him to a new district and a new set of surprises.

By this point in his career, Dan understood that panicking and running down to stand over the support folks did nothing to make the troubleshooting go faster. It was better to remain calm, get periodic updates, and be prepared to handle any questions as they bubbled up. Meeting with Christie's administrative staff, he proposed that whenever a third-level escalation arrived in the future, Christie's secretary would intercept it and immediately transfer it to their "acting" district level, Mr. Graham. That procedure worked perfectly for months until, one day, an E911 Center circuit failed and a third-level escalation found its way to Dennard's secretary. She promptly transferred the call back to Graham's office where his secretary answered and explained that Mr. Graham was away from his desk. The call bounced back to Dennard's office, and she angrily accepted it and promised to "Get to the bottom of this!"

Dashing down to Graham's office, Dan's secretary sheepishly told Dennard that Graham was unavailable. "Well, where is he? I have an escalation here and I need him right now." Dan's secretary haltingly explained that he was in the restroom. Without responding, Dennard turned on her heels and found her way to the men's room. Dan was in one of the stalls when he heard the main door open and a shrill voice ringing out, "Graham, are you in there?" Before Dan could reply, she continued. "I have an escalation and you need to get out here and handle it."

Dan yelled back, "Please leave it with my secretary! I'll be out in a moment—as soon as I finish the paperwork!"

The story of Christie invading a men's room spread throughout the CPC quickly. Many of the workers found it humorous but not surprising. They generally viewed Christie as harmless, but most dismissed her as just a bit too quirky. They felt she came across more like a character in a play rather than a serious operations department leader. Their assessment intensified each time they observed her dealings with Harvey, her pet rabbit. She very publicly spoke of the animal much as a mother would discuss her child. Daily she would entertain her staff with a new Harvey escapade. She explained how she prepared special salads for him, bought birthday gifts for him, and set up special playtimes with other little bunnies. Rumor had it that the animal's cage alone cost her over $1,000. She even had a speakerphone installed near it, rigged to answer automatically so she could listen and talk to Harvey every day at lunchtime. One Easter, she

6

A Buddy, a Wheelbarrow, and Two Meltdowns

Randy Hanes was imminently likeable, always had a smile on his face, good-natured, and appeared to be a real "people person." He was also the most difficult boss Graham ever encountered. Graham learned to put up with Cy Greene's strange baseball behaviors, Steve McKinney's intimidation strategies, Burt Larkin's bullying, and Christie Dennard's panic attacks. No one *ever* figured out a successful approach when working for Randy. Randy needed you to believe he just wanted to be your "buddy." Those deceived by the façade soon learned otherwise.

Like Christie, Randy was unaccustomed to dealing with a union workforce. Unlike Christie, however, corporate rumors suggested that executives had *not* sent him to the CPC for grooming but for punishment. Randy had fouled up some important strategic plan budgets, which created major problems at state headquarters. The vice president ordered him removed to a distant location where he would cause no harm. Next stop: the Circuit Provisioning Center. Hanes understood that Dan's groups were operating efficiently under Dennard's former regime and so left well-enough alone. It did not end there, however, as he had big plans for the district. Randy was entirely disinterested in the CPC operations; to him, they were boring, complicated, and beneath his dignity as a former strategic planner. He desperately wanted to find some way to get back into the good graces of the higher executives and searched for his opportunity to bring attention to himself.

Hanes was a *flavor of the week* kind of leader. A voracious reader, he devoured popular management and business books constantly, usually reading one a week. Recognizing that Graham was finishing his doctoral studies, Hanes called him into his office every Monday morning to discuss his latest insights. Unfortunately, many of them seemed to conflict with the concepts proposed in the previous week's tome. Nonetheless, Hanes was always eager to try some leadership technique he had learned the night before. Regrettably, he rarely implemented them in the right circumstances with the right personnel.

Hanes could quote chapter and verse from any of two dozen popular management books. He knew that some theorists described leaders who focused mainly on their tasks while others emphasized personal relationships. He understood that some workers were only motivated when a boss stood over them while others enjoyed the work itself, never needing close supervision. He could explain how some employees required specific directions while others wanted personal coaching. He also read that a select group enjoyed participatory or empowering leadership. He could recite theories explaining how some responded best when the boss fully delegated tasks and never interfered. Too often, however, Hanes tried to match a management technique to a situation that called for an entirely different approach. In fact, he rarely considered the *readiness* of his workers and erred by choosing the most "enlightened" style in the most inappropriate circumstances. He tried, for example, to fully delegate projects to very inexperienced employees and faced disastrous results. He assigned hardnosed union workers to *self-managed* teams and was stunned to find they could not accomplish their objectives without closer supervision. Randy just came across as a wide-eyed idealist who thought everyone would just work productively after singing "Kumbaya" and engaging in a group hug.

Understanding Randy's tendency to generate complications, Dan tried to keep him away from his groups because he usually stirred up some unexpected problem. After reading about the advantages of employee empowerment in certain situations, Hanes was determined to find an opportunity to experiment with the concept. Regrettably, he decided to try the approach late one afternoon when he ambled down to the DAB group. There, he found JW working furiously while guiding field crews as they restored service to thousands of customers. A damaged cable carried hundreds of special circuits and JW was ensuring that each was reconnected and restored properly. Graham knew that JW was more than capable of handling this type of problem and was one of the most conscientious managers he had. He also knew JW would stay well into the night to make sure the crews completed the job. As usual, Dan was prepared to stay with them simply to offer support. When these emergencies occurred, Graham always saw his job as removing barriers and supporting the human needs of his support team. He made sure they got a break every hour or so, he ordered their lunch and had it delivered, and he handled any other simple duty so they could remain focused on the problem.

Observing the organized chaos, Hanes gradually realized that the work activities were efficient and productive. Dan was checking on the progress when Randy heard a temporarily frustrated JW complaining that the process was taking forever and he was threatening to "hang up, shut down the computer, and go home!" Dan knew JW well and realized this outburst was simply a technique to get the attention of one of the field workers who was likely ignoring his advice. Overhearing the threat, however, Hanes misinterpreted the remark and—remembering his empowerment book—seized this precise moment to "teach" a profound lesson on "sophisticated" leadership.

Intervening, he directed JW to place the workers on hold and meet with him for a few minutes in the conference room along with Graham. JW looked to Dan for approval to leave the phone and they both scurried into the meeting area. "JW, I know it's after 5:30 so if you really want to leave now, you are certainly empowered to do so. I want you to know that

I'll respect your decision. I know that as a good manager, you'll choose to do the right thing." Randy felt that he was showing JW that he just wanted to be his "buddy" rather than his director. He sat back, confidently predicting that JW would feel honored that his "good friend," the director of the entire district, expressed so much trust in him.

"Mr. Hanes," JW asked, "are you sure you would let me leave in the middle of this problem?"

"JW, I trust you on whatever decision you make," Hanes reassured him. "I'll leave it entirely up to you, no repercussions." At that point, Dan intervened and reminded Randy that they were working on an important problem and he did not appreciate the interference. "Dan, wait a minute. Let's just see how JW handles this opportunity to take responsibility for his own decisions without a boss telling him what to do." JW turned to Graham and with an implied wink, stood, thanked Hanes for the chance to exercise his own judgment, and headed into the hall toward the elevators.

Graham glared at Hanes and could not hide his annoyance with Randy's interference. "He's headed home," Graham grumbled. "That's why I've just about ordered you to stay away from my people while they're handling problems. We had this under control until you came down here with your management experiments. How's that working out for us now?" Without waiting for Randy's response, Dan hurried down the hall to catch JW at the elevator and entered with him.

Nothing was said as they rode down together. JW broke the silence as the elevator opened to the first-floor lobby. "Dan, you know me. I'm not really leaving. I just can't believe this guy comes in and disrupts everything just to make some silly management point. I'll have a smoke and be back up there in a few."

Randy had retreated to his office by the time Graham returned. JW returned after a much-needed smoke and had the service restored by 6:30 p.m. Graham offered a simple thank-you as they walked to the parking lot together. It was all JW needed to hear to know how much Dan appreciated him.

When Dan reported to Steve McKinney years ago, he observed a very interesting fact. McKinney could collect 80 percent of the information he needed, quickly weigh the pros and cons, and then make a major decision. Steve knew that his decisions were sometimes wrong, but that fact never discouraged him from being decisive. To an executive responsible for hundreds of millions of dollars, *timely* decisions were often more important than *perfect* decisions. Less decisive leaders waiting to dig up that last 20 percent would forever face missed opportunities. Randy, on the other hand, needed that 20 percent. It represented closure. He was deathly afraid of making a bad decision on just about any issue, perhaps because of the reputation he earned in the strategic planning department. Consequently, Randy delayed many of the district's important activities by forcing employees to scramble around at the last minute attempting to uncover some obscure fact. He wanted precisely 100 percent of the data necessary for his decision-making process. Thus, when higher management advised Randy to prepare a "dog and pony" show for the new president of operations, his tendency to indecision nearly paralyzed him.

Finally, after fretting over the assignment for hours, Hanes called Dan into his office and explained that the district needed to have an impressive presentation to wow their new president. Hanes reported that the new president scheduled a tour of the operations districts, and the CPC was second on the list with a four-hour appointment in two weeks. While Randy had no idea what to do, he said, "Look, Dan, I know you can really write some quality *bull s**t* so I want this guy leaving here with very positive feelings about the CPC's top-notch leadership and important contributions to the company's service standards." Hearing Randy's backhanded compliment about *BS*, he reminded Randy that one of his (Dan's) most important roles was making his leader look so good that he or she got that coveted next promotion. Graham knew that was a bit of an exaggeration, but he truly approached a task like this with that in mind.

Dan thought he knew exactly what he needed to do. He formulated the marching orders in his mind. "Make good old Randy look great, and just maybe they'll promote his butt and get him out of here!"

He tried to get some more detail from Randy, but being his usual indecisive self, Hanes just kept saying, "I'm really not sure. It could be a set of slides, a notebook of facts, or some sort of scripted presentation by each of the second-level managers. You decide and show me a few days before the big show." Graham assembled a small group of managers and administrative personnel and began the task of collecting facts. They mapped out a slide presentation and a comprehensive handbook of facts and outlined brief presentations to involve the other second-level managers. They completed and published the materials and coached the supervisors on their presentations. All aspects of the presentation pointed to one inescapable fact: *the CPC performed extremely well thanks to Randy Hanes, a great leader.* Four days before the event, Dan and the four supervisors met Randy in the conference room for a preview.

After the forty-five-minute performance, they waited for Randy to exclaim, "Well done! Let's go with it!" A minute passed as a pained, *indecisive* expression appeared on Randy's face. "Guys, I'm not really sure this is what we want. I'm still not exactly sure how it should look, but I think I'll know it when I see it."

Dan and the team, experienced with presentations like this, knew it met all the parameters a higher executive needed to see. Their production even managed to make Hanes appear competent, a stretch for anyone who knew him. Dan saw this as just one more example of an indecisive leader *delegating* when he should have *directed* or *empowering* when he should have offered *coaching*.

Attempting to control his frustration and recognizing that they would need to start from scratch just days before the event, Graham stood and addressed all of them. "Randy," he said as calmly as possible, "in two days, I am rolling a wheelbarrow into your office. It will be full of our presentation materials. I am going to dump it on your floor, and you will look at it and tell me that it is perfect. Now exactly what do you see there?"

After a few snickers from the supervisors, Randy agreed to outline where he thought Dan should update the materials. The approach had forced Randy into making decisions that might affect his career. It was a very painful process for him. The team was relieved to find that his recommended changes were relatively minor.

The day of the big show arrived. The new president had a reputation for being an hour early for meetings so every manager in the CPC was in early. Dan had arrived at 6 a.m. for the 9 a.m. meeting. While doing some last-minute prep work, his phone rang. Looking up at the clock, he was curious; he rarely received a call at 6:30 a.m. Picking up the phone, Dan listened as a breathless voice erupted, "Hey, Dan, Randy here. Listen, I'm at the turnpike exit on Sample Road. My car overheated so I jogged the last mile to use the tollbooth phone. I need you to come and pick me up."

It turned out that his car had a leaking radiator, a repair that Randy kept delaying because he could not make an important decision: trade it for a new car or simply have it repaired. Just one more indecisive moment in his life. Instead, he added water every morning for a month while he worried over the issue. The leak progressively worsened. On this most important day, he left early and *forgot* to fill the radiator! He agonized over what to do when he smelled the car overheating. He decided to press on at seventy miles per hour, convinced he could get to the office before any permanent damage. That was clearly the *wrong* decision. The engine seized and came to an immediate halt. At least the engine's meltdown, he thought, had helped him with his decision to buy another car.

Dan left immediately and drove twenty minutes to pick him up. They pulled into the parking lot and observed the president and his entourage preparing to enter the building. The president had seen Randy arriving late for work, chauffeured by one of his supervisors as if he were royalty. The look on the president's face said everything; no explanation needed. It simply confirmed the rumors he had heard about Hanes: a mistake-prone leader constantly needing attention. Randy was beside himself, appearing to experience a meltdown much like his pitiful engine.

Although their "dog and pony" show went well, Randy knew that the initial impression was not favorable. He was even more desperate for some sort of project to gain positive attention. Randy's penchant for ignoring assigned responsibilities to focus on side projects evolved soon after that meeting. From his readings, he learned about the management system du jour: Total Quality Management (TQM). Although W. Edwards Deming documented the process some four decades earlier, it was all the rage in corporate America about that time. Randy was convinced that if he could implement it in his CPC, the executives would finally recognize him as the forward-thinking, pioneering leader *he himself* saw when he looked in the mirror.

The corporation was also involved in making other important changes at the time, including a major reengineering effort that would soon affect Randy's little empire. He somehow schemed to delay that by wrangling a deal that merged his CPC with several other statewide districts, an effort aimed at circumventing the reengineering project entirely. He then recruited Graham to begin implementing TQM in the merged centers. Hanes had already become so involved in TQM activities that he was chairing statewide meetings on the process. Dan subsequently transferred all his work groups to Ray, one of the supervisors from the merged districts, and began the task of installing TQM.

Randy, resuming his "best buddy" persona, wandered down to Graham's office a few days later to offer some advice on the TQM project.

"Dan," he said, "I just wanted to caution you about this one union president I've been working with over the last year. I think you will find him to be your stiffest challenge. So far, I haven't been able to get through to him. They call him 'Sammy the Snake.' The name says it all!"

Sammy the Snake Haley was, indeed, feared by most managers throughout the region. Randy had faced *the Snake* (as everyone called him) several times while presiding over the state TQM conferences. Randy described Haley as an imposing figure at six-foot-six with a permanent scowl and personality to match. After meeting him once, everyone understood how he got the nickname. Whenever Randy tried to employ his *I'm-your-buddy* strategy, the Snake made it painfully clear that his friendship was neither accepted nor desired. "So Dan, you're going to need Snake's buy-in to get this TQM implementation moving. I don't envy you. I just hope you can get it handled."

Dan was not looking forward to the meeting they had scheduled. Driving the fifty miles to visit at the union hall, Graham repeatedly practiced his speech to convince Haley that TQM was the right thing to do. He planned to explain a few benefits the union members would enjoy: better training, more input to work decisions, and more realistic measures that could help to refocus their supervisors on systemic problems rather than a bunch of random worker errors. Nevertheless, Graham was not at all convinced he would emerge unscathed.

Wearing his *I'm a manager* white shirt and tie, Graham received some unfriendly glances as he entered the union hall. He walked through a very large conference room with a few cafeteria-style tables and fifty or sixty folding chairs stacked on the back wall. He rounded the corner and saw a nameplate on an office: "S. Haley, President." Gathering his courage, he tapped on the open door and walked confidently into the large office, holding out his hand for a welcoming handshake.

"Danny, Danny Graham, that can't be you!" an excited Snake proclaimed.

Looking stunned, Graham responded, "Silly—I mean Sammy—er, Mr. Snake? I didn't know—I didn't recognize—"

"It's been—what?—twenty, twenty-five years?" Haley interrupted.

Sylvester "Silly" Haley grew up around the corner from Graham. From the time they were ten years old, they played sandlot baseball and football and got along famously. Back then, Haley preferred the nickname "Silly" as a diminutive form of Sylvester, so Dan never imagined that Sammy the Snake Haley was actually Silly Haley.

"Well," Haley volunteered, "I guess Silly never gave me the right image after I grew up, and I couldn't go by Sylvester. When I started working here, I decided to call myself Sammy 'cause it starts with an *S*. Then, when I ran for union president, I added *the Snake* for a little color. It worked. Just look at me now!"

After reminiscing awhile, the two agreed on some fundamentals that would appear beneficial to both the union and management. They shook hands after an hour and Haley said, "I think I can sell this TQM stuff to the members my way. Anyway, Danny, I'd invite you for a beer but it's probably best we aren't seen together down here."

"Understood," Graham said as he left, still amused and amazed at one of the luckiest coincidences he could ever remember. On the long drive home, Dan thought again about how his old friend Lady Luck just kept showing up at the most unexpected times in his career. He felt a bit of a grin trying to form.

Graham returned to his office late that afternoon. Eagerly awaiting his arrival, Randy intercepted him in the hallway and asked, "So how did it go?"

"That is one tough guy!" Graham exclaimed. "I was lucky to get out of there alive!"

"Yeah, but what about—"

Dan interrupted. "We got everything we wanted." He never revealed the old friendship that sealed the deal. *Some things your boss just doesn't need to know,* he thought as he confidently strolled back to his office.

Not long after that episode, Hanes needed to complete annual performance reviews for his existing second levels as well as the recently inherited supervisors. Ray had worked with Dan well over a decade earlier in Steve McKinney's staff group. In those days, Ray maintained an impeccable reputation as the regional expert on the company's computerized trouble tracking systems. He was about twenty years Dan's senior and Graham frequently sought his advice on operations issues. Now some fifteen years later, Ray's reputation had faded. He occupied a low-profile supervisory role and the intensity and enthusiasm he once possessed was a distant memory. Frankly, upon seeing Ray again for the first time in years, Dan was a bit surprised at how Ray had settled into this low-key role. Nevertheless, Ray remained a solid performer and valuable supervisor if not a superstar vying for the next promotion.

Hanes called Dan into his office several days before appraisals were due and said, "Dan, you know Ray better than I do. He seems a bit laid-back. What's your opinion of him?" Graham explained how Ray had once been on the fast track to higher management but was derailed when the company changed computer applications and operating systems. Dan acknowledged that Ray seemed to have lost some "fire" but cautioned that Randy should not underestimate him.

"He's very intelligent," Dan insisted. "He can handle any situation you throw at him and puts enough effort into his job to always turn in a good performance. He's not quite as flashy as he once was, I guess because he's eyeing retirement now."

Immediately after Hanes met with Ray on his evaluation, Ray hurried down to Dan's office, invited himself in, and slammed the door. "So what's the purpose of you undermining me with Hanes?" Graham started to ask what he meant as Ray interrupted. "He rated me a low performer in several categories. When I challenged him, he said *you* concurred and told him I was really a poor performer compared to the old days. Thanks a lot. What a crock!" Ray left the office without waiting for the true story. From that point forward, however, Dan knew that he could never trust Randy again. Dan's relationship with both Randy and Ray deteriorated from that point on.

Graham's TQM installation was starting to deteriorate as well. Dan had always suspected his efforts were futile, as he knew corporate leaders were intent on ramming through the reengineering projects despite Randy's protestations. He was right. After about three months, Randy received orders to *cease and desist* with his mergers and quality programs. The reengineering consultants entered the district a week later and made it clear they were in charge. They immediately ordered Graham to change direction and work with them over the next eighteen months as they built an entirely new center. Named the System Infrastructure Support Center (SISC), it was much larger with regional responsibilities compared to the CPC's smaller footprint. Hanes began to embrace the concept as he finally saw his opportunity for glory, convinced that he would get a chance to direct a modern kingdom.

One of Dan's responsibilities during the project was to visit the new vice president of operations for the state, Steve McKinney. McKinney was Graham's former boss and Randy's new boss. During that visit, Graham observed the same arrogant style he endured fifteen years earlier. McKinney then did something entirely unexpected. He confided in Dan, "I'm planning to replace Randy when you get this SISC up and running. I don't want to leave him in there fouling things up. Now you keep your mouth shut on that. I'm telling you because I need your help to make this work." Steve knew that Randy's interest in TQM had actually caused some notice at headquarters, where they were still emphasizing the system. "I intend to get Hanes so hung up in TQM that headquarters will ask for him. Then he's gone! You just keep doing your best to make him look good. I'll do the rest."

Dan remembered that Burt Larkin's transfer to headquarters a decade earlier was just such a scheme. Randy's targeted job appeared to be an excellent opportunity for him to achieve corporate wide visibility and grooming for a promotion. Instead, it was a secret plan for executives to confirm all the rumored flaws. Randy's fate was sealed.

McKinney's scheme almost fell apart a few weeks later when Hanes entered Graham's reengineering office and closed the door. "Look, I know you and McKinney have a history together. I know you worked for him ten or fifteen years ago. I have a big problem and need your advice." Randy proceeded to explain how, in the monthly staff meetings with the other operations directors, McKinney berated him, antagonized him, and bullied him. In a word, Steve was employing his standard intimidation technique. Dan quickly realized this sounded like a facet of Steve's hidden plot to make Hanes uncomfortable so he would jump at any chance to transfer.

Instead of revealing that information, Dan explained that Steve often reverted to his college football experience as a linebacker. Back then, he tried to intimidate his opponents until they completely avoided him on the field or finally stood up for themselves. He found it a very productive tactic, too, as he ascended the ranks in the company. "So you're saying I should just stand up to the guy and call him on it?"

Dan agreed. "Yes, something like that." Dan pointed to several examples, including himself, where Steve gained respect for a manager when that person finally refused the bullying tactics.

"Good. That makes sense," Randy said. "You know, I played linebacker in high school until I was injured so I know all about intimidation. I'll settle this once and for all." Dan heard the response and cringed. He wanted to tell Hanes that Steve was just looking for some assertive leadership rather than fear and retreat. Graham knew that Steve responded well to a courteous but confident dialogue. Randy, on the other hand, seemed determined to trigger a major conflict. Dan could not imagine how Steve might respond to an insolent confrontation. He chose to believe that, surely, Hanes would exercise good judgment when they clashed.

He was wrong.

Three days passed and Dan realized his worst fears. Hanes barged into his office cursing and accusing Graham, "You set me up! I confronted him just like you said, and he went off like a nickel rocket. I don't know if I'll ever recover from that."

Dan asked what had happened, and Randy explained that when Steve started one of his intimidating tactics, Hanes got about two inches from McKinney's face and yelled that he was tired of the pressure and threats. He said the situation quickly deteriorated from there. Dan tried to say he could not understand how Randy utterly misinterpreted the advice, but Hanes stormed out of the office. Dan could not hold back a chuckle and a knowing smile. He heard nothing more about the incident from Randy or McKinney for several days.

Entering the building a week later, Steve stopped him at the door, and they spoke of job offers. He knew something was up.

7

The Top Ten Jobs List

"Graham, I want you to come work for me as chief of staff after your taskforce is completed," the vice president of state operations barked and then turned to walk away without waiting for an answer. As he and Dan approached the entrance to their headquarters building, McKinney stopped, turned back to face Graham, and said, "I have some news about your boss, too!"

At first, Dan was at a loss for words. He had worked for Steve some fifteen years earlier and did not find it a pleasant experience. Then a director, Steve was an up-and-coming leader in the company and had just returned from a tour at corporate headquarters. He exhibited the infamous "Triple A" management style: abrasive, abrupt, and arrogant. Graham was convinced that he left a poor impression with Steve that first time, so he was reluctant to embrace the offer. Before he could gather the words back into his mouth, he blurted, "That's not on my top ten list."

"See me in my office. It will be the best career decision you ever made," McKinney said as he continued to walk away without turning to face Dan.

Dan was a second-level manager completing a major reengineering assignment. He had no employees—just taskforce leadership duties—but previously led departments of ten supervisors with a hundred nonmanagement employees. Typically, second-level managers reported to directors who led departments of five to ten second-level supervisors. The VP confronting him had ten directors with 7,000 nonmanagement employees and some 1,500 supervisory personnel in the state. He wielded a lot of power in everyone's eyes.

Later that day, Graham gathered his courage and visited Steve's *old-school* executive secretary. With the persona of a head librarian, Mrs. Sinclair was stern, authoritarian, and decidedly quiet. She exuded a professional aura reminiscent of a bygone corporate era and Dan understood that she did not tolerate loud, talkative visitors in her professional domain. In those days, corporate executive secretaries brandished nearly as much authority as the senior managers they served. In quiet, reserved tones, Graham asked Mrs. Sinclair to announce his presence. McKinney overheard and bellowed, "Come on in!" while Sinclair rolled her eyes at the inappropriate summons.

The office was magnificent, yet McKinney's larger-than-life personality seemed to fill the entire 1,000 square feet of space covered in finely crafted wood paneling. It was brimming with beautiful, expensive executive furniture, a significant departure from the open workspace cubicles in which most of his 1,500 management employees labored. He had decorated the walls with professionally framed pictures, certificates, and awards detailing his accomplishments. A wall nearest his desk featured a favorite framed photo. It documented the moment he signed a scholarship with a famous college football coach twenty-five years earlier. As Graham entered, McKinney swiveled his chair toward the built-in credenza and flipped a switch. Thirty feet of curtains began to close slowly but deliberately, darkening his twelfth-floor windows and obscuring their view of the Intracoastal Waterway.

To be sure, Dan had visited the office several months earlier while working on his current reengineering project. Outlining the proposed changes in operating procedures, Dan sought Steve's formal approval for the new workflows proposed by his taskforce. Before that first visit, however, several peers forewarned Graham about Mrs. Sinclair's prickly reputation, so he called ahead requesting an official appointment. Upon arrival, he adopted the expected quiet, reverential demeanor in her presence. He was careful to greet her in hushed tones and engaged in courteous small talk while waiting. That interview went well, but Steve displayed his usual arrogance, taking delight in making a veiled threat that Graham's *inside operations* reengineering project "had better not" degrade the support his *outside operations* department expected. He then reminded Dan that he had once told him, "Graham, you're exactly the kind of guy I'd shove into the wall every time I passed him in my high school hallway. Don't forget it."

On this, his second, visit at McKinney's directive, the automated curtains startled Graham as they began their journey. Steve instructed him two or three times to sit before Dan's attention turned back to the impending meeting.

McKinney immediately launched into his pitch, clarifying what Dan would be handling as his chief of staff. He did not start with "Have you changed your mind?" He simply assumed Graham already agreed and proceeded with the explanation. McKinney reminded him that his reengineering project was ending and, as an aside, pointed out that Dan was one of eleven managers displaced by the reorganization. "You know," he said, "only five of you will remain with us after this."

As one of the new district's designers, Graham was well aware of the required reduction in second-level managers. From the eleven managers in the merged districts, only five were required to operate the new SISC. The company's reduction plan was common in corporate America at that time. It involved a forced ranking process, mockingly referred to as *rank and yank*. Several executives, including McKinney, would rank the eleven managers on numerous performance and leadership characteristics. Those with the five highest scores would remain. The lowest six would receive an offer for early retirement. Dan knew that the probability of any one of the managers remaining in the company was less than 50 percent. On the other hand, Graham was slightly more confident than the others were. He knew all the official raters and they understood that he was the only manager involved in the design process. He had also unofficially placed his name on one of the internal SISC groups to reserve a possible future slot after the project ended. None of the eleven, however, felt assured about their future as they had seen previous rating systems end with unexpected, disturbing results. One of the older managers, recognizing that an early retirement offer might include considerable monetary incentives, began a personal campaign by wearing a lapel button inscribed, "Rate me low and let me go."

Despite Graham's understanding of the process, Steve's "only five" comment somehow triggered a flashback to a meeting between Graham and McKinney well over a decade before. When Graham worked for him all those years earlier, Dan was the acting supervisor of a group of senior engineers, left in charge for several months by a reassigned manager. Upper management had earmarked the vacant position, reserving it for another supervisor rotating back after a special assignment at headquarters. McKinney had just returned from headquarters as well, inheriting Graham as an interim supervisor. He summoned a much younger Graham after a couple of days on the job. As Dan entered Steve's office, much more modest than his VP headquarters some fifteen years later, Steve skipped the greeting and said, "Let me tell you about the two managers I fired last month for failing to do their job!"

This caught Graham by surprise. He did not hear much after that. He felt the need to defend himself but awkwardly reminded his new boss that he was merely filling a temporary vacancy in the org chart. He reexplained that he was the same level as the other team members and lacked formal authority from an official job title. Still stunned by the opening remarks, the only comment he remembered was that McKinney expected a more forceful, less quiet management style. His suggestions came across as orders. Graham returned to his office quite shaken. To complicate matters, McKinney was preparing Dan's year-end performance evaluation just a week after that meeting, so as a twenty-nine-year-old manager attempting to climb the corporate ladder, he was convinced his career was derailed—perhaps doomed forever. When they met later to discuss the evaluation, Steve had checked the box labeled "Not Promotable" supported by the handwritten comment "This manager is too quiet; needs to develop a more forceful management style."

At first, Graham accepted the rating and comment at face value, recognizing that McKinney described him quite accurately. He had long acknowledged his tendency to introversion but worked diligently to overcome—or at least disguise—the trait. While he knew one's fundamental personality was an unchangeable characteristic, he found ways to improve his quiet demeanor to develop a more acceptable, forceful style in the workplace. Then, rechecking the company's guidelines on rating employees, Graham confirmed his suspicions. Corporate evaluation policies stated that management *style* was the least important factor in the performance review. The most important was the leader's effectiveness, determined by the performance of his or her group in meeting measurable results. Dan prepared a quick memo respectfully explaining that perhaps Steve had misinterpreted the corporate policies and should avoid filing an evaluation that could highlight his misunderstanding of the guidelines. He then offered an analysis of his group's results and explained how, despite his quiet management style—and despite having no formal authority over his group—they still exceeded every measure. He sent it and prepared for the worst.

A day or two went by but Dan heard nothing. Then the call came. "Meet me in the conference room." When he entered, McKinney was sitting on a stool facing an empty stool placed about two feet away. When seated, Graham was close enough to feel that Steve was purposely invading his personal space as he sat knee-to-knee with the former college linebacker. "I read your memo," he said, "and I've updated your evaluation. Sign here." That was all he said. Graham quickly looked at the form and found that McKinney had prepared a new page, eliminated the handwritten comment, and checked the box "Promotable Now-One Level." Dan signed, left the meeting, and they spoke no more of the incident. Six months passed before Graham's promotion came, making him one of the youngest engineering supervisors in the company.

Pushing aside the memories, Dan forced himself to refocus after the "only five" comment. The next words he heard were "By the way, Randy is out of here. Got the paperwork signed today. He'll oversee Total Quality for the entire company. I guess I should thank you for the help in that. Let's see how long he lasts!" While he was pleased to hear how Steve had handled Randy's job, Graham was more concerned about *his own* job working for McKinney. Dan was looking forward to assuming a nice, quiet role as one of the five remaining SISC second levels. Instead of responding directly to the offer, Graham guardedly reminded McKinney of their confrontations years ago. He then explained how upset he was at the threat the first time and confessed that he had vowed *never* to accept another position with Steve. McKinney was surprised to hear the revelation and quickly addressed the misunderstanding, trying to explain his true intent.

"You misunderstood. I was just trying to empower you—to let you know I had your back if you wanted to give a swift kick to a couple of those senior engineers in your group back then. I just thought you were a bit too quiet in confronting them. I felt they were slacking off and that you needed to be more forceful. I was suggesting that you should threaten them—intimidate them a bit—by pointing out how I handled a similar situation!"

Dan finally realized that the original misunderstanding stemmed from his declining listening skills after McKinney mentioned firing someone. He then asked McKinney about the possibility of hard feelings on the evaluation challenge.

"Let me tell you something," he said. "You did me a favor. I rechecked the policies myself and I'm glad you caught me before I documented that error. You recall that I never admitted my mistake, don't you? Well, I did. Make a mistake, I mean. I can do that now; I've changed a lot. Back then, you were one of very few managers who had ever challenged one of my decisions and stood up to me. I respected that but never acknowledged it. So why do you think you were promoted so quickly after that? Where do you think you got the support? And why do you think I want you to come work for me now?"

Dan did not respond to McKinney's questions as it suddenly occurred to him that Susan Petroskey, a former CPC manager, currently occupied the chief of staff job. Instead, he changed the subject altogether and blurted out, "So where is Susan going?"

"Promoting her. She's backfilling Randy in the new SISC you're designing," McKinney said in a matter-of-fact manner.

It all became clear at that moment and Dan accepted the job. However, he had still not heard the entire story. As they stood to shake hands and seal the deal, Steve revealed the most important fact in the selection process. Grasping his hand firmly, Steve gave a little tug, pulled Graham toward him, and said, "Besides, you were the *only* manager Mrs. Sinclair approved of. She told me flat out she wouldn't work with any of my other selections. Said you were the only manager who ever came up here and was polite, professional, and—most important—*quiet!*"

Six months passed, and McKinney hurried down the hall to Dan's new office. As he rounded the corner, Dan heard him bellowing, "Hey, Graham, listen to this." He then read from a prepared announcement in a sarcastically officious tone.

> Randy Hanes, director of the Corporation's Total Quality Management Initiative, announced his retirement today. Please extend your best wishes to Randy as he enters a new adventure in his life.

8

A Chief, but Which Doctor?

"Graham, didn't you say you're finishing a doctor's degree?" McKinney asked.

"Yes," Dan responded while seated in the visitor's chair in front of Steve's enormous desk.

"Didn't you say Barry Westenhoff was in some of your classes?"

"Yes," Graham confirmed.

"Well, I guess he finished his degree, right?"

"Yes," Dan replied once again. "What's up? Why do you ask?"

McKinney then explained that he called Barry's office a few minutes earlier and Westenhoff's new secretary answered. Before she could greet him, McKinney said he needed to speak to *Barry*. Not recognizing McKinney's voice, the secretary corrected him in a haughty manner, saying, "Sir, he has instructed that everyone is to address him as *Dr.* Westenhoff from now on. Whom shall I say is calling?"

Rather than responding, McKinney hung up and summoned Graham to his office.

McKinney held an MBA, earned about the same time Graham was reporting to him fifteen years earlier. While several engineering managers and ex-spacemen held master's degrees, Graham and McKinney were likely the only two in the company's south operations divisions with MBAs back then. McKinney continued to rise in the company through the Management Development and Evaluation Plan (MDEP) and had no time for additional schooling. Dan, on the other hand, pursued an advanced degree when the company encouraged a return to college as downsizing all but prohibited upward mobility. Dan had started classes eight years before, just after reporting to the CPC. With his dissertation all but complete, he expected to earn his diploma within six months. Dan revealed these facts during his first week as Steve's chief of staff and McKinney openly admitted that he was jealous. "In fact," McKinney offered, "don't ever expect me to call you *doctor*. That just *ain't gonna* happen!"

"So watch this, Dan," McKinney said as he redialed Westenhoff's office a few minutes after the first call. The secretary again answered the phone.

"Dr. Westenhoff's office. How may I help you?" She had meticulously enunciated his title, as if to educate the caller on the proper way to address her boss.

"This is *Mr.* McKinney. You tell *Barry* to be in my office in one hour!" The emphasis he placed on his words were meant to counter the inflections Barry's secretary had voiced. McKinney was making it abundantly clear that he had no intention of ascribing doctoral status to her boss. As he hung up, he told Dan, "I think you're going to like watching this!"

Graham knew that Westenhoff's office was about ninety minutes away even with light traffic on the interstate, so he expected the new doctor's tardiness would help to ignite the opening fireworks. Just as he found himself excited to observe the confrontation, he realized that he really had no desire to witness the massacre that was about to occur. Making up some excuse about finishing the project he was handling, Dan excused himself and left Steve's office.

Graham knew Westenhoff's reputation through the company, of course, but also knew of him as a fellow doctoral student. Barry was a military academy graduate who failed to achieve the next promotion in rank, opting out per the military's *up or out* philosophy. He was also stagnant in the company, passed over several times, and apparently stuck forever as a district manager. His leadership style was inflexible as he approached every task as though he were in a combat zone. Regardless of the situation or readiness of his workers, he delivered orders and expected immediate, unhesitating obedience. His dissertation topic revealed much about his inner conflicts. It was a scholarly indictment of methods for assessing military officers and corporate executives. Sentence by sentence, he constructed a solid case examining how managers with "outstanding" leadership skills were often underestimated and ignored. The comparisons to his personal situation were undeniable.

When Graham heard that Westenhoff was arriving, he could not resist the temptation to overhear what was happening. Since Mrs. Sinclair was out for the day, Dan took a seat in her visitor's chair outside McKinney's closed door and pretended to work on some unidentified tasks. Try as he might, he heard nothing. Ten minutes had elapsed when the door opened abruptly and, without speaking, a red-faced Barry swiftly headed down the hall to the elevators.

A minute later, McKinney appeared at the doorway and said to no one in particular, "Well, I guess *that* took care of *that!*"

"So what happened?" Graham asked.

"We had a difference of opinion over several topics, including whether I would call him *doctor.* I won," McKinney bragged. "We'll need to start looking to backfill him. He's sending in his official resignation as soon as he gets back to his office."

"Boss, just for the record, I will forever be plain old *Dan.* No titles."

"Good, let's keep it that way," snapped McKinney, showing just a bit of pent-up disgust he should have directed at Westenhoff ten minutes earlier.

Before his unceremonious "retirement," Westenhoff was looking forward to participating in a long-awaited customer satisfaction project. With his newly minted degree, he was sure he could impress the prestigious consultants and, perhaps, parlay his contributions into a job offer with their prominent firm. Believing he was too talented to remain in the lowly telephone industry, Steve granted his wish just a bit too soon as the distinguished professionals entered the picture a few months later.

It was a well-known fact that Steve hated consulting firms. In the giant telecoms, most consultants arrived in an operating district only to uncover inefficiencies that would lead to head count reductions. By analyzing the level of inefficiency, headquarters could simply identify and impose the lowest force needed *if* the district were operating efficiently. Then the district leadership would have to figure out how to survive while getting everyone up to speed with 20 percent fewer workers. As a result, many a career was derailed, and McKinney knew it.

It was with this in mind that Steve, three months after Westenhoff's resignation, confirmed the imminent arrival of the prestigious consulting firm Mackenzie and Company. After investigating, however, Steve realized this was not the standard consulting firm on a "seek and destroy" mission. Intent on improving customer satisfaction and earning the J. D. Power Award in that category, the company chose McKinney's region as the field trial for improving Customer Desired Due Date (CDDD) and Same Day Trouble Repair (SDTR) results. Both strategies correlated directly with customer satisfaction, an area in which the company was underperforming. McKinney prided himself on knowing, as he said, "which levers to pull," so he already knew that he simply needed more workers to hit all the targets. Persuading higher management to authorize a larger customer repair workforce, however, would require consultant buy-in. Convinced that the internal measures already proved his outside techs were operating quite efficiently, Steve invited the consultants in with open arms. With all the paperwork ready to sign, he eagerly awaited the go-ahead to requisition a couple of hundred additional personnel when they concluded their study.

Steve summoned Dan one afternoon and assigned him as liaison to the consulting firm with a mandate to make sure their two hundred additional crew members materialized. Graham answered, "No guarantees, but I'll try my best."

Steve shot back, "Not the answer I wanted to hear. You are already planning your concession speech if you're not successful." He continued.

"By saying that, you can simply explain away any failure by telling me you didn't guarantee success but at least you tried. That's just plain bull—! You need to show some confidence. Make me feel like you are up to the task!"

Dan suddenly understood he had used this approach his entire career. Not wanting to have someone count on him and then fail, he always chose to hedge his bets by telling his boss he would simply try hard and, if he failed, at least he would avoid accusations that he misled his supervisor.

Steve then said, "Look, you've heard me tell my boss, 'I'll handle it. Consider it done.' With that, I have set my supervisor's mind at ease. I've also established a hard target for myself so I'll try even harder to handle a difficult task, knowing that I never even implied I would fail. What's the worst that could happen then? I'm telling you it's better to reassure your boss than formulating some excuse in advance."

Graham thought for a moment and responded, "I'll take care of everything. We'll have those two hundred techs. Count on it." As expected, the consultants soon confirmed the need for additional workers. Dan was relieved; he was never actually convinced he could make it happen.

After several weeks, the firm called a major meeting of the state's divisional leaders as well as Vice President McKinney and his boss, the company's president of operations. The agenda included a discussion of force additions and an outline of plans for a trial of their proposed policies. As the meeting commenced, Mackenzie's lead consultant, Dr. Gupta, stood to introduce his associates and the onsite consultants who had worked on the project. "To my left are Dr. Rogers and Dr. Fellowes. On my right are Dr. Grossman, Dr. Kendrick, and Dr. Gonzalez."

McKinney, hearing all the titles among his guests, stood and announced, "Well, that's an impressive crew you have there, Dr. Gupta, but I have my *own* doctor on staff. This is Dr. Graham. Last week he received his doctorate in business administration. We *all* call him *Dr.* Dan around here."

To everyone's surprise, Gupta and his associates all stood and offered polite applause. Graham felt self-conscious but nodded in appreciation. From that moment, with McKinney's lead, all Dan's colleagues and every one of McKinney's upper-level peers referred to Graham as *Dr.* Dan. McKinney never discussed the abrupt change, but Graham concluded that Steve got a kick out of bragging that he had a doctor working for him. He might have remained a bit jealous, but Steve seized every opportunity from that point forward to underscore Graham's degree when introducing *his* doctor.

"Dr. Dan, come on in here. It's training day," Steve said when Graham answered the phone a week later. One of the tasks McKinney always reserved for himself was grooming his management team for future leadership positions, so he invited his subordinates to observe how he handled various situations. Steve had already used these sessions to impress upon Dan a number of issues he needed to analyze and track. McKinney also made sure that Dan understood one of the more important topics he considered when rating his division managers' competence: their customer trouble load. Each division had a limited number of repair personnel and a daily log of several thousand complaints requiring a field visit. Heavy rains always generated customer trouble reports and every operations leader placed a premium on "handling today's load today." If, on the other hand, their force-load equation began to get out of balance, everything failed. The overtime payments exceeded targets, expense levels shot up, and customer satisfaction indices plummeted. More important, every manager from VP on down to the local supervisor came under increasing scrutiny to rein in the unacceptable conditions.

During Dan's early morning staff meetings with Steve, McKinney often took a moment to call around to his less experienced division managers just to check on their general progress. His usual greeting included the question "How many troubles did you open up with this morning?" McKinney, of course, knew the answer before he asked. The first report he reviewed as he sat down every morning was the daily load report. It included a list of every division and every repair dispatch location. It showed the number of troubles on file at 6 a.m. plus the number of repair technicians scheduled to work that day. It also offered a ratio reflecting the number of troubles assigned per worker. Most repair personnel could complete seven to eight dispatched troubles per day. If the load increased to ten per worker, the division manager usually authorized overtime to catch up. If weather caused the ratios to exceed that, the division managers consulted with McKinney to authorize a temporary personnel loan from another division.

Graham jogged down the hall and took a seat in McKinney's office, wondering what little leadership stratagem he would witness that day. He understood that the occasional *training day* was sometimes for Dan's benefit, sometimes for the benefit of another of McKinney's direct reports, and sometimes for both. When Dan learned that they would be dealing with Ben Forrest, Steve's newly promoted division manager from another state, Graham suspected a lesson aimed at stressing the importance of their daily repair strategies. Forrest had little experience in operations when he took over the central division, so he was unfamiliar with many of the job's requirements. As Dan watched, Steve called to quiz Ben with his standard *how-many-troubles* question. Forrest answered quickly, "Not sure, boss. I'll check on that and call you back."

McKinney hung up after some pleasantries and, turning to Dan, said, "Wrong answer."

A couple of days passed, and McKinney asked Dan to sit in again. "Hey, Ben, what's your load today?" Steve asked.

Again, Forrest answered, "Not really sure on that, but I did have another issue I wanted to share with you." Steve listened politely to Ben's concern but reminded him to call back as soon as he had the trouble load answer. McKinney glanced at his watch as if he were documenting the time elapsed before Ben's response.

The following day, Dan watched once again as Steve made his third and final call to Forrest. He began with some generic banter before casually mentioning, "By the way, what's your load today?"

Suddenly sensing his third failure, Ben chuckled nervously and explained, "Well, you caught me again. I'll check and call—"

McKinney interrupted him and snapped, "You had exactly 2,974 troubles at 6 a.m. That includes 137 held over from yesterday. You have 381 techs on the load this morning. That's 7.8 troubles per worker. Now I think you should have figured out that I already know the answer when I ask about this. You also need to realize that, whether *you* think it's important or not, your *boss* thinks it's important. I suggest you don't ever let it happen again."

It never did.

Owing to his success with little "training exercises" like this, Steve found comfort when focusing on measurable tasks rather than the higher leadership demands like communicating strategic vision and direction during tough economic times. In fact, despite his apparent control in every situation, McKinney remained an inexperienced vice president who had not fully embraced his role. He had huge responsibilities with a $1 billion budget, 8,000 workers, and a dozen division managers. He knew he needed to start viewing big-picture duties while finding a way to rid himself of the daily *security blanket* tasks he embraced instead. To be sure, McKinney had finally moved beyond the intimidation strategies that served him so well in his formative years, replacing them with habitual checking, rechecking, and double-checking a dozen detailed reports every day.

Since neither of them knew exactly what Graham's job duties *should* entail, Steve took the easy way out by instructing Dan to collect daily reports from the division managers. He wanted travel expense reports for individuals attending out-of-town training, overtime reports on individuals earning higher overtime payments, trouble load reports, daily budget updates, and a series of other up-to-the-moment indices. All of these arrived on McKinney's desk by 8 a.m. every morning. He thumbed through them, circling a number here and there. After thirty minutes, he bundled the two-inch stack of papers with a large rubber band and scribbled an "S" on the top document. When Mrs. Sinclair entered his office an hour later, she removed the bundle and headed directly to the shredder, feeding in all the documents for several minutes.

Clearly, McKinney's increased scrutiny on overtime pay and travel expense caused grumbling among his several thousand union workers. However, he assured a general uprising when he started focusing on inefficient repair personnel who were not meeting tasks-per-day expectations. Strolling into Graham's office early one morning, Steve said, "Graham, come with me downstairs for a little visit." While looking out his twelfth-floor office window, McKinney had just seen a group of union members from the Telecommunication Workers of America (TWA) congregating near a truck parked in front of the building. As they walked across the parking lot toward the gathering, they observed an old pickup truck surrounded by sign-carrying union members. McKinney started to chuckle when he saw the contents of the truck bed. It was an expertly made, life-size replica of a wooden hangman's gallows. Dangling from the noose was a full-sized dummy with a large sign pinned to its chest. As Dan and Steve maneuvered to read it, they finally saw one word. "McKinney." Many of the protestors also held professionally lettered signs saying, "McKinney unfair to TWA workers."

"Stay here, I'm going to have a little chat," McKinney ordered.

Dan remained at a distance as Steve approached the union's local president leading the group on the sidewalk. Graham looked for a handshake. None was apparent, but the confrontation did not appear hostile. After a few moments, McKinney turned and walked back across the parking lot toward Dan. At the same time, the group threw their signs into the pickup and began to disperse.

"So what did you say?" Graham asked.

"Nothing much," McKinney explained. "Just made sure they saw me. I just had to be the figurehead leader they needed to antagonize. I allowed them to complete their little mission. They'll be leaving now to head back to the union hall so they can brag about their confrontation with the *head man.*"

Graham understood that all these reports, including identifying inefficient repair technicians, were important and needed reviewing. What he did not agree with was having this checking and rechecking task sent up the line for handling by a vice president. Dan believed that the boss should always delegate down the org chart, not absorb responsibilities best left to his or her subordinates or subject matter experts (SMEs). In fact, Dan always tried to manage according to the old military document given him by John Voorhees when he was still a junior engineer. Called the "Doctrine of Completed Staff Work," it explained how a general officer must rely on his reporting staff to handle high-level jobs. Graham pulled out the old, dog-eared copy occasionally to share with *his* subordinates. He always emphasized the paragraph stating,

> It is your job to advise your chief what he ought to do, not to ask him what you ought to do. He needs your answers, not questions. Your job is to study, write, restudy, and rewrite until you have evolved a single proposed action—the best one of all you have considered. Your chief merely approves or disapproves ... [this way] the chief is protected from half-baked ideas, voluminous memoranda, and immature oral presentations.

Dan also believed Steve needed to embrace "managing by exception," the classical technique wherein the boss avoids decisions on every issue, addressing only issues that truly get out of line. Indeed, Graham knew from his TQM training that management should always consider the effects of Statistical Process Control (SPC) before reacting to every minor bump in a process. That approach was not only unproductive but risky as well. In fact, the tenets of SPC suggested that focusing excessive attention on the individual blips of *in-control* processes could seriously upset a system that was otherwise performing normally. Nonetheless, Steve's micromanagement approach generated a comfort zone wherein he felt safe. He simply substituted the familiar checking behaviors for the higher-order activities his position demanded.

Finally, one of the senior general managers privately asked Dan to help him *manage their boss* by persuading McKinney to drop the constant reporting. The line organizations were spending an inordinate amount of time on unnecessary details. Tracking every penny of a few hundred dollars in travel expenses, compared to a $500 million expense budget, seemed an unnecessary waste of their time. Graham agreed to undertake a "one-man" effort to illustrate to the VP that his focus on manual tracking reports was adding nothing to the bottom line. He intended to show they were counterproductive and inferred the GMs could not be trusted. After some time, Dan convinced McKinney that the experienced GMs deserved to have a number of these responsibilities delegated to them. Graham pointed out that the GMs would remain accountable for meeting their budgets (they were all very experienced) and that McKinney would merely have to check progress on the official automated monthly budget reports that Dan volunteered to review for him. Although met with resistance at first, Steve finally recognized that this was likely the best way to manage the business at a high level. Both he and Dan began to observe that the GMs became even more focused on their expenses and indices after realizing they could not delegate their responsibility "up the line" to a higher checking authority.

Beginning to change his strategies, Dan and his colleague Karl Simskey pressed the VP to become more visible to his "troops." In short, they insisted that Steve "get out there and lead." Karl suggested he needed to stop using his reports to find only the *negatives* needing punishment and, instead, find the *positives* deserving a reward. Karl then proposed bonuses for the management teams in work centers exhibiting the best workforce efficiency measures. They worked out all the details and within a month had a stack of $500 bonus checks for a local management team.

"Come on, boys. We're going to play Santa Claus," McKinney said late one morning.

Dan grabbed the checks and threw them in a briefcase, and the three left for a thirty-minute ride to visit one of the work centers at lunchtime. Having called ahead to have the managers assembled for a meeting, they had no idea what was up. To date, McKinney had only visited locations like this when they were underperforming. Most of them probably expected a stern speech with one of his infamous warnings like "Look to the left. Now look to the right. One of the three of you won't be with us if this doesn't improve!"

Instead, Karl gathered the people into a meeting room and McKinney walked to the front to address them. "I'm here because this is the most efficient work center in the state, and I want to congratulate you. Oh, and by the way, I have a little token of the company's appreciation. Dr. Dan, what do we have for these fine folks?"

Graham, in an exaggerated ceremony, opened the briefcase he had placed on the table in the conference room. "Here you go, boss," he said as he walked to the front and handed over the envelopes. Steve started calling names, having the people walk to the front to receive a check as he shook their hands.

On the ride home, Steve was beaming. "We gotta do this again."

Karl agreed and responded, "Got it, boss."

It turned out that reports pointed to the same work center as the most efficient just six months later so the three of them piled into the company car for another enjoyable experience. This time, the team knew exactly what to expect so they gathered quickly without Karl's encouragement. Most of the managers had already earmarked their bonus for some much-anticipated purchase. As before, the team enthusiastically received their envelopes and shook McKinney's hand. The whole team gathered outside to wave as the three drove off.

As fate would have it, the work center fell out of the top spot six months later so it was no longer eligible for a bonus. Since they were only a short drive from his building, McKinney thought it might be a nice gesture to visit the work center anyway just to reassure them that finishing in second place was still a remarkable achievement. Unfortunately, he had already conditioned them to receive rewards, so Karl cautioned that they would be expecting something more than a pep talk. McKinney suggested that was nonsense and headed to the car with his two staff members. Of course, the visit was anything but enjoyable. Like puppies trained to expect treats when they saw their master, all the workers gathered when they saw McKinney's car pulling through the gates. The group listened politely as Steve spoke, but the disappointment on every face was undeniable. "That didn't turn out so well," McKinney remarked as they drove toward his office. Karl started to say that he had tried to warn him but always knew when to keep his opinions to himself.

While Graham worked on the in-office strategies, Simskey kept pushing for McKinney to expand the field visits he had started. Steve still countered, insisting that his monthly staff meetings served that purpose. He would repeat his common refrain "Too much work here in the office to get out and wander around talking to people." As McKinney's delegating strategies began to take hold, however, that argument no longer rang true. Finally, Karl saw an opportunity to get a commitment to hold a series of annual conferences to talk to all 1,500 managers face-to-face. Karl convinced him that he would take care of all the logistics and provide the data McKinney needed to discuss while Dan would line up guest speakers and prepare McKinney's personal presentations. Steve allowed them to set it up once, and he loved it. He was evolving from an intimidating manager to an enlightened twenty-first-century leader skilled at communicating with workers at all levels.

Dan and Karl proved repeatedly that effective staff managers needed to manage their boss while practicing the doctrine of completed staff work. Just as important, they also knew it was sometimes appropriate to disobey the boss while, at others, it was essential to comply. This came to a head when Steve's new president of operations directed him to prepare a business plan for the state. At first, McKinney told him he and his staff were too busy for that kind of needless work. McKinney then recounted the subsequent exchange. "So he asked me what I was doing at four o'clock in the morning. I told him that I was still in bed, of course.

So Alfie comes back with "Exactly! Maybe you should start your day a little earlier if you don't have enough time to run the business!"

McKinney thought for a long contemplative moment then added, "I just don't like the guy!" Dan and Karl were almost sure they heard several curses surrounding the new president's name as Steve walked away muttering to himself.

As Steve told the story about getting to work on time, Dan thought back to the first week he reported as McKinney's chief. Dan prided himself on getting into the office before his boss so he was there at 7:30 a.m., knowing Steve would arrive around 8 a.m. McKinney finally asked him after a week, "What time do you get here in the morning?"

"Before you," Dan answered.

"Well, I'll be in here earlier tomorrow," Steve shot back. "You're not going to beat me in!"

Dan thought the little contest just stemmed from Steve's competitive nature, so he accepted the challenge and arrived at 7 a.m. the next day.

McKinney pulled in at 7:15 a.m. "I'm in even earlier tomorrow, Graham," he said as he walked through the office suite.

The following day, Dan arrived at 6 a.m., convinced that Steve would not beat him. Nearly two hours passed, and McKinney never appeared. At 8:35 a.m., McKinney sauntered through the door and greeted everyone, never mentioning the contest. Following him into the office, Dan said, "Wait. You didn't comment on how I beat you in again. Admit it, boss. I won!"

"Oh yeah, what time were you here?"

"Before 7 a.m.," Dan shot back with a huge grin. He wasn't expecting McKinney to bow humbly while admitting defeat, but he was hoping for some sign of contrition.

"Good. Let's keep it that way," McKinney barked. Dan suddenly realized he had been "schooled." Clearly, McKinney just wanted his staff arriving early and staying late. It was an effective method to teach the lesson without issuing an imperial decree.

Beating his chest as if he were a dominant silverback gorilla, McKinney bragged, "So never mind that Alfie boy told us to submit a business plan. I need to train him; he needs to understand that *I* run this place without any of his guidance *or meddling!"* Watching McKinney's little display of power and authority, Graham started to argue and warned that Alfred would ultimately order him to do it anyway.

"Then," Dan said, "you'll come in here and stick me with a last-minute emergency assignment."

Steve insisted they would not comply under any circumstances. "Don't worry. We aren't doing it. Clear?"

With a mock salute, Dan said sarcastically, "Yes, sir!" and strolled out of his office.

Of course, Dan and Simskey began collecting data immediately and then called the president's staff to identify the proper format. Christened the *Word-man* and the *Data-man* by McKinney, Dan and Karl prepared all the material despite Steve's orders to the contrary. They knew the president wanted the plan by Friday, so by Thursday, they had a two-inch-thick, bound report with narratives, colorful graphs, and data tables. As predicted, McKinney came through the door Thursday afternoon and sheepishly admitted he was wrong. He needed the plan. "Sorry. See what you can do."

"We'll get right on it, boss. Don't worry. Count on us." Dan and Karl tried to contain a chuckle as they glanced at each other.

Steve sensed in that response that something was up, but he simply turned and headed to his office. They waited a full five minutes before marching into McKinney's office to hand him the completed plan. Realizing they had disobeyed his direct order, but thankful they had, Steve said absolutely nothing. He reached out, took the bound booklet, and ritualistically held it on the fingertips of both hands like a serving platter. Then standing, he dropped it from three feet above his desktop. It made an agreeable, heavy thud as it fell on the desk and whooshed stacked papers everywhere. "Not heavy enough. Go put some more stuff in it and let's ship it out." As the two headed for the door, he yelled at them, "Thanks!"

They grinned as they left the room.

Still trying to manage their boss, a few months later McKinney became curious. "What are all these posters I keep seeing around here? A six-digit number taped in the elevator; I get off and the same number taped every ten feet down the hall. I walk into my office, and here are a couple in my drawer and one on my desktop. What are you guys up to now?" Neither Dan nor Karl revealed anything.

Two days later, Steve called down to their office. "OK, I see the new maximum salary levels authorized for second levels. I get it. And you *won't* get it!"

When Steve handed Dan his salary increase printout a month later, Graham was delighted to see the familiar six-digit number.

Karl called Dan half an hour later. "That *manage your boss* thing is working out pretty well, I'd say!"

One of Graham's jobs as chief and official word-man was occasionally writing rationales to promote one of McKinney's second-level managers to a district level executive position. "Dr. Dan," he would say, "you're the only person in this entire company that writes as good as I do. Now go make it happen!" As a promotable second level himself, Graham was always a bit annoyed that he was constantly making his rivals appear so appealing and worthy. All vice presidents like Steve took pride in placing managers from his or her region into leadership positions throughout the company. McKinney developed a reputation for being one of the best at it. He had a handful of district levels and division levels from his state populating the headquarters staff and other regions in the company. As such, he was always able to call in a favor or dig up some obscure information to stay one step ahead of his top VP rivals or his boss.

Recalling that McKinney had promised the staff job as his best career decision, Graham began to wonder, after about seven years as chief, if he would ever get that next big career step. While preparing a promotion package for the next candidate, Jim Miller, Dan slipped in an "unauthorized" rationale for himself as well, just to see what would happen. In it, he summarized his service highlights and the promises he heard over the years. He described how many of his former mentors had retired so that most of his significant career achievements were no longer on the radar. He compared himself to the five most recent candidates he helped to promote and, in each case, showed how he (Dan) was equally capable or even more qualified for an executive position. He also threw in McKinney's memorable way of explaining the need for a mentor. "Everybody needs a *daddy* or a *mommy* to guide him or her up the ladder." Pointing to that quote, Graham boasted in the document that he had the best mentor in the business for the last seven years.

After signing the paperwork for Miller, Dan asked to speak to McKinney privately regarding a career decision. Upon entering the office, McKinney quickly told him, “I read your little manifesto. Some good points. So noted.”

“Thanks,” Dan said, “but I just want you to know I have developed a fairly serious self-esteem problem after helping all these others to get promoted.”

“No, no, no, I don’t detect that at all. You have certainly transformed from the quiet, shy person I supervised over twenty years ago. I don’t see that you have *poor* self-esteem at all!”

“Boss, that’s not what I said. I have a self-esteem problem for sure, but it’s not *poor* esteem. Basically, I think I’m *better* than all these folks we’ve promoted over the last few years. In fact, I believe you know that too! You’ve told me I’m the best chief of staff you ever had, and I guess that’s part of the problem. I don’t think you want to lose me here. As long as I’m politicking for a job, here are my campaign promises: When you promote me, I promise to continue handling all your official correspondence. I promise to prepare your promotion packages. I promise to write your performance evaluations to make sure you get those big raises. I also promise to continue creating your conference presentations and speeches. I promise all that along with whatever job I’m promoted into.” Graham stood and left quickly after his little speech, hoping that McKinney did not detect how nervous he was. He knew that he had sealed his fate one way or the other.

Some six months later, Steve walked down the hall to Graham’s office while holding an official memo. Entering the office, he stood in front of Dan’s desk with a small group of staffers gathered there and read,

> Effective May 1, 2002, Dan Graham is promoted to director—System Infrastructure Services Center (SISC).

> Dan joins the senior management team from an executive support position on the network vice president's staff. He replaces Susan Petroskey, who recently announced her retirement. Since Dan will continue with his executive support responsibilities, his staff position will not be backfilled. Dan's background includes tours in outside plant engineering, transmission engineering, network technical support, and centers operations. He holds bachelor's, master's, and doctor's degrees. Please welcome Dr. Dan to the state leadership team.

Graham was not at all surprised by the announcement. He had written it for McKinney a week earlier.

9

The Whac-A-Mole Conspiracy

In the early 2000s, as the newly promoted director over six hundred workers and fifty managers, Dan was learning a new lingo. In a company that placed a premium on acronyms, his System Infrastructure Services Center (SISC) was an amalgamation of multiple work units previously located in a dozen regions under a similar number of directors. He spent a week relearning the names and functions of his new charges. The AFIG, CPG, TCG, OCO, EBAC, MATV, SASS, RCMAG, NFC, and CTG were all distinct groups that somehow worked together under one umbrella. Dan's SISC workers sat before computer terminals nine hours a day programming software and offering support for local, long-distance, and high-speed internet services.

While working on the corporate reengineering project several years earlier, Graham had helped to devise the plans for work centers like this, never thinking the company would promote him to direct one of them someday. As a precursor to the *offshoring* many businesses were pursuing, Dan's company spent enormous sums uprooting workers and building huge centers in each southeastern state, hoping to gain economies of scale through consolidation. Graham and the other reengineering planners organized the work so that all the technicians in a specific regional center did essentially the same type of work. Unfortunately, when all the similar work functions migrated into nice, neat centers, an alphabet soup of stand-alone groups remained. They had very little in common other than they all performed some behind-the-scenes role in delivering telecommunications service. Like the unused letter tiles remaining at the end of a Scrabble game, the reengineering folks dumped all the leftovers into a big box called the SISC. Dan's multiple SISC work groups inhabited three buildings on both ends of the state, some three hundred miles apart.

With a generous $35 million operating budget, Graham was planning for some stability while he learned the finer points of performing as a new director. He and his reengineering colleagues had designed the center well and it was already operating smoothly so he expected to settle into an uneventful job. He was looking forward to enjoying a little down time as a fifty-year-old executive making his last stop before early retirement.

He was wrong.

Within weeks of taking the new job, headquarters summoned Graham and the other four regional SISC directors to a meeting announcing a new round of reengineering for the centers. The work involved a twenty-four-month consultant-led project that guaranteed a reduction of the center's workforce by 30 percent. No one believed the claim, but Dan knew it would affect the lives of some two hundred people in his district even if only partially true. This was certainly *not* going to be the nice preretirement job he imagined.

Headquarters had hired a newly formed consulting group incorporated as Business Partners Inc. (BPINC) to install a new Administrative System for Operating Control (ASOC). Mockingly referred to as the *Be Pink* group, their marketing team had convinced top telecom executives they could deliver enormous efficiency improvements. ASOC involved some rather old-school concepts coupled with sophisticated new computer applications. Borrowing from the early days of scientific management's use of time and motion studies, the BPINC consultants proposed to analyze every work process performed by the alphabet soup groups. Over 1,200 activities and process flows would require formal flowcharts, after which a SISC manager would conduct statistical timing studies for each activity. Finally, the SISC managers and *partners*, as the consultants called themselves, would develop expected standard times and load them into the computer. The ASOC system would then track each worker's progress while completing daily work routines. From this, their computer applications could prepare efficiency reports for each worker and display them on a real-time monitor placed on each supervisor's desk. Reports for all the alphabet groups were also summed into a three-tiered rating for the whole SISC. It showed how the entire center was performing—moment by moment—as workers attempted to reach targets for 100 percent efficiency, 90 percent utilization, and 90 percent productivity.

Early in the implementation stages, Graham attended an ASOC conference at headquarters to challenge the system's fundamentals. He explained that the alphabet groups in his SISC did not enjoy consistent, steady workflows that could allow managers to balance the force-load equation. SISC leaders could not manage the unionized workforce in a manner similar to the forlorn seasonal migrant workers serving the state's agricultural industry. The service order volume (load) fluctuated seasonally, but union rules prohibited cyclical workforce adjustments that could match these changing levels. He pointed to data showing that the middle of his state saw a huge influx of order activity in August as 50,000 university students returned to dorms and off-campus apartments in an otherwise sleepy little town. In the southern part of the state, another massive invasion exceeding 800,000 retirees began after Thanksgiving and ended at Easter. These so-called snowbirds "flocked" to the region where they owned condominiums and mobile homes or leased apartments. Establishing head count efficiencies based on the enormous volume in August or November would result in significant inefficiencies a month or two later. To drive home the point, he proposed a farcical analogy by suggesting that if BPINC's analysis team visited a local fire department, they would find firefighters polishing the fire truck or watching TV in their lounge. Stressing the flaws in the process, he suggested that BPINC's computer program would reach the erroneous conclusion that the overstaffed station required an immediate firefighter reduction. His point was simply that they had not programmed ASOC to account for discontinuous work activities, nor was it capable of dealing with major seasonal variances. Dan's staff and the BPINC group politely listened to his concerns and replied, "So noted." It was simply a more courteous way of responding to unwelcome suggestions in his company at the time: "If we want any *bleep* out of you, we'll squeeze your head!" Nothing changed.

The partners and managers reviewed the ASOC reports weekly to identify training opportunities for the entire workforce. The initial lack of adequate progress resulted in remedial training programs. If a worker did not improve, the supervisors initiated the union's four-step discipline procedure. First, the employee received *counseling* and the supervisor entered a formal notice into their personnel file. With inadequate improvement, the supervisor made a *warning* entry. If the employee still failed to meet the requirements, they were *suspended*. Finally, after extensive grievance proceedings, Graham was required to *terminate* for failure to perform. Although he rarely had to take an employee past the warning stage, there was extensive pushback from the union (Telecommunications Workers of America). The management team balked, too, since everyone faced significant change to his or her management style. Soon, the supervisors began to anticipate a reduction in management as well, especially if the 30 percent reduction materialized. Near rebellion ensued. Employees—management and nonmanagement alike—began openly mocking the project with the slogan "Be efficient, be productive, but *never be pink!*"

As the de facto leader, Dan had no choice in liking or disliking the project. He understood the importance of lowest cost operations for competitive reasons. He had already seen a number of other centers of this type forced into off shoring so there was very little wiggle room. Two issues, however, made matters even more uncomfortable. First, the upstart BPINC leaders drove the project ruthlessly since it was their first major ASOC installation. They had literally tied their compensation and future to its success. To finalize the contract, they *guaranteed* the implementation time frames as well as the major force reduction projections. To the partners, that meant *no savings/no pay*. Second, as a newcomer to the consulting arena, the company had few full-time resources and only hired personnel after they secured the contract. The rapid ramp-up resulted in a steady stream of unqualified, uninformed "partners." They served a month or so providing inept guidance to the alphabet groups until BPINC dismissed them. Accordingly, SISC teams spent weeks collecting complex data only to dump it and start again when a replacement consultant introduced himself or herself on a Monday morning.

Lead consultants were sent to every SISC to supervise each local team of a dozen partners. Working closely with Graham, Harry Clemons was decidedly competent with an impressive background in leading large projects, but he also expressed frustration with the inexperienced personnel dealt him. Excessive BPINC turnover and poor support threatened to capsize the entire project. Expected to conduct 7 a.m. training sessions each Monday for the district's management team, Harry privately confided that he rarely received the instructional materials in his email before 4 a.m. that morning. Nonetheless, the consulting group exhibited very little compassion for the human element in the process and focused wholly on the numbers, driving nearly impossible schedules for completion. The whole system seemed broken.

BPINC executives required Harry and the other four lead consultants to issue weekly scorecards rating the district's general attitude toward the project. Called the "Red-Yellow-Green Report" ("R-Y-G"), it was secretly prepared and sent to the highest corporate executives without the knowledge of the SISC directors. Harry privately advised Graham that he (Dan) was already on BPINC's watch list owing to his VP's previous reputation with consulting groups. McKinney had expressed open opposition to the ASOC project from the beginning, insisting he would "play by the rules" only if his SISC director confirmed that the meddling consultants were *not* getting out of line. "If Dan reports any problems," he warned, "all bets are off!" Graham knew he was now in the direct line of fire. He also knew he could not publicly express disagreement with the project. While McKinney could get away with grandstanding on the issue, Graham was a newly promoted director facing a career-ending predicament.

With the exception of a single positive experience with McKenzie and Company, Steve had a long history of clashing with consultants. His empire featured some 8,000 workers and a $1 billion budget. McKinney developed and guided it with little or no input from intrusive consultants over the years. When they did show up to greet him with "I'm from headquarters and I'm here to help," Steve brusquely escorted them to the exit. Central to Steve's dislike of consulting groups was the knowledge that they consistently focused on finding inefficiencies and thus always recommended force reductions. To divisional presidents in most corporations, employee head count was a sacred number. Any threat to their workforce levels became an implied threat to them personally.

Graham recalled an earlier time when a lead consultant met with McKinney to "review" his strategic planning group, a disingenuous approach aimed at uncovering an excuse to reduce personnel. McKinney believed that consultants, while useful in auditing operations, could never justify their value unless they characterized insignificant problems as major issues needing corporate attention. Steve had already read the consultant's report on another planning district. It identified numerous minor issues to paint a picture of incompetence and neglect. The conclusion strongly suggested a head count reduction. McKinney's meeting started with polite exchanges but had an undercurrent of tension. Finally, in a dramatic move by a vice president who had spent a lifetime intimidating his adversaries, McKinney leaned in very close and quietly said, "You are welcome to report on my strategic planning district. Now this is not a threat. It is a promise: If your report is slanted to make any of us look bad, I'll find you and I'll reach into your chest and rip out your still-beating heart!"

Two weeks passed before the consulting firm issued an outstanding evaluation. Force reductions: *none.*

If Dan embraced ASOC wholeheartedly, McKinney would likely berate him for not standing up to the "agitators." On the other hand, if he complained too intensely, he would wind up in the Red Zone of the R-Y-G report, and the higher executives would have their say. So he walked the tightrope, trying to appease both sides. By showing measured pushback to BPINC, he attempted to curry favor with McKinney and his own management team. At the same time, he worked effectively with the consultants behind the scenes to eliminate implementation roadblocks. That kept him off the R-Y-G hit list. One of his first jobs was to convince the union leadership that he would be fair-handed and act in the best interests of the workers. He and the union agreed that the first task would center on identifying adequate training for all the workers who were having problems, a big union agenda item. He committed to formal training for his workers, giving them every chance to succeed. He further committed to begin quarterly retirement opportunities as many of the workers were already late in their careers and looking for incentives to leave.

"Declaring a surplus" was the bargained-for force reduction process documented in the TWA working agreement. Over twenty pages of precise rules detailed the official procedures management had to follow to administer force reductions. All SISC leaders had to understand every nuance to avoid unwanted union grievances. Dan determined that he could offer early retirement packages that featured a year's pay in addition to their regular pension. Many SISC workers were actually looking forward to this chance. He collaborated with union leadership to encourage workers to consider these offers, a move that could help to avoid displacing personnel early in their careers or those needing to continue to work. They began the long process of judiciously implementing these early retirement incentives while matching force reductions to efficiency improvements.

While successfully "removing" ten or fifteen employees per quarter seemed to be a very aggressive approach, Dan secretly knew that achieving a reduction of two hundred workers was still an unrealistic goal.

When Dan served as McKinney's chief of staff, they developed the slogan "Communicate, communicate, communicate. And when you think you have communicated enough, communicate some more!" He carried this admonition with him as he approached the ASOC challenge. He understood that a successful implementation would hinge on his ability to face the affected workers and discuss the project. He did not expect his workers to embrace the message, but he thought it might buy him some credibility and perhaps a small measure of respect. In fact, after several meetings, most were impressed that their district leader would personally visit and face the critics.

His union leaders told him privately, "You know, our last director never would have done this. She always hid in her office and just issued orders." This comment clicked with Dan, and he knew he needed to be even more visible during these stressful times. Realizing his tendency to introversion, Dan forced himself to assume a more social persona and launched his *management by walking around* (MBWA) strategy. He wandered through his buildings as often as possible, greeting the workers and engaging a few in brief conversations. It was not a pleasant task at first, but the workers warmed to the process and looked forward to his brief visits.

As hoped, his approach seemed to resonate with the workers as some acknowledged, "Well, at least this guy has some integrity."

Dan's arduous task of holding work group meetings continued with the union leadership in attendance to answer detailed questions about *surplussing*, the company's shorthand term for processing the excess (surplus) workers. At one point, his union counterpart pulled him aside and good-naturedly warned him, "Dan, make sure you always check behind your car tires when you back out of your parking space. A handful of roofing nails can make a mess of your tires." Graham had heard of these tactics to register disapproval of managerial polices, so he began his habit of checking behind each tire before leaving.

By the fourth formal meeting, Dan was beginning to feel comfortable explaining the nuances of the project and graciously fielding the hostile questions. On the sixth meeting, he noticed that the first two women entering the small auditorium were dressed entirely in black with hats and veils. A few men then entered, dressed in dark suits, starched white shirts, and black ties. Dan saw these same workers daily in their T-shirts and jeans, so their appearance caught his attention immediately. As the fifty members assembled in the room, he looked out on congregants dressed for a funeral. The symbolism was not lost on Graham, and it made an indelible impression. It changed forever the way he interfaced with his workers.

When ASOC began, declaring force reductions based on efficiency improvements each quarter was a difficult process that no one welcomed. Dan knew that he could never proclaim ASOC a success until the supervisors began to *request* that Dan declare surpluses to meet their efficiency commitments. At the beginning, he issued top-down decrees, a rather authoritative approach whereby he simply told each group how many people to remove each quarter to meet the numbers. It was a poor way to operate, but at the time, Dan's management team was not convinced they could survive with fewer employees. Moreover, a few first-level managers simply refused to abide by the new job methodologies. Dan used the performance review process to either convince them to change their habits or seek retirement as well. On the other hand, many first-level managers began adopting the strategies and enjoyed the resulting efficiencies.

After a year, supervisors did start approaching their second-level managers *requesting* surplus declarations. Dan no longer had to issue imperial decrees; he could simply wait until his first levels volunteered to reduce their own force. He had only to prepare the paperwork to meet their wishes. The process finally began delivering all it had promised. Moreover, Dan had somehow achieved the perfect balance between McKinney's force planning strategies and BPINC's demands. During a lavish corporate award ceremony, headquarters selected Dan's SISC as the most improved infrastructure center in the company and McKinney beamed with pride at the attention, recognizing that Graham's success was a positive reflection on him (Steve) as well.

Of course, union leadership retained its defiant attitude in public to maintain the proper image but admitted behind closed doors that they were satisfied Dan kept his word. For the most part, the folks who chose to avoid change were happy to leave when offered early retirement packages. Overall, 90 percent of the district's personnel left in a manner favorable to their personal plans. Those who remained began the slow but sure task of adapting to the new process and Graham's district became the corporate model for successful ASOC implementation.

Unfortunately, the complications did not end there. It was not enough to participate fully in all the analysis activities; the program had ascended to near cult status. Recognizing that most SISC groups were still missing their scheduling targets and jeopardizing BPINC's compensation agreements, the *partners* stepped up their tactics by establishing a particularly onerous certification program. To assure compliance by all parties, BPINC published certification procedures that included the statement "Certification demands that an organization *emotionally embraces* the ASOC philosophy."

After reading that, Graham could no longer contain his anger and challenged BPINC to define precisely how they expected to measure his team's level of emotional embrace. He mocked the policy, asking if they were planning to implant electrodes and run encephalograms to develop an emotional embrace quotient (EEQ). He insisted that since ASOC was based on precise measurements, he wanted them to define exactly how high the ink line must jump to register *satisfactory* or *better than satisfactory* emotions. The firm was not amused, and Graham was reminded that his behavior was very close to earning a career-damaging appearance on the R-Y-G report. It also triggered a stern warning that such heretical thinking would call into question his SISC's dedication to ASOC's fundamental principles. It was clear to many that the BPINC group seemed to be morphing into a cult, complete with their sacred scriptures and warnings that any deviation could lead to eternal damnation—or at least to the R-Y-G report!

At that point, the program took on a life all its own, creating a significant growth opportunity for headquarters support groups. The corporate staff added numerous members to write continuous updates to ASOC policies. They hired others to conduct field audits aimed at certifying every district once or twice a year. The constant attention kept everyone in strict compliance with each group in lockstep, no deviations tolerated. Confident that his district was now the model for ASOC success, Dan began to feel that he could no longer ignore a nearly totalitarian regime that quashed any critical thinking about the process. When his best managers started devising better workflows, BPINC summarily dismissed their ideas by insisting their revisions would not meet certification requirements. Finally, in an act of defiance, Dan summoned the courage to start publishing his "Friday Morning Rants" to point out the absurdities his managers experienced but were afraid to express.

In a preblog environment, Graham started to release an email featuring a page of angry outbursts every Friday morning. Sent to his SISC team colleagues and certain higher executives, he highlighted some aspect of an ASOC system gone horribly awry. In the first sentence of his first rant, he wrote, "ASOC is a tool that gets us to where we need to be … not an end in itself. It needs to be invisible and working for us, not constantly bringing attention to itself like some misbehaving child." With that single statement, BPINC immediately placed him in the R-Y-G Red Zone while fellow SISC directors and his own management team applauded. Dan could not quite grasp how he had gained the courage, but he knew it was the first time someone challenged the mystical BPINC gods rather than bow and appease them with human sacrifices, although he would soon believe *he* might be that sacrifice.

Not long after Dan started his Friday missives, he received a *Harvard Business Review* article widely distributed by one of the higher corporate executives. It discussed the attributes of great leadership and concluded with an admonition that corporations must engage in succession planning by identifying valued traits in the next generation of leaders. Dan had observed many of these favorable characteristics among his SISC supervisors, but each time they took the lead in offering an innovative ASOC refinement, they met harsh criticism from the certifiers.

Observing the worsening situation and realizing top executives were insistent on developing leaders—not interchangeable parts in an industrial machine—Graham finally saw his opportunity to blow the whistle. He published the rant that, some suggested, eventually led to BPINCs downfall. He likened the emerging ASOC compliance strategy to Whac-A-Mole, a trademarked arcade game in which furry little creatures pop up from holes while a player attempts to smash them directly on the head with a mallet as quickly as they appear. He ended his rant with "I consider our senior leadership to be a first-class team able to think on their feet and accept change to remain relevant. Had they started in this hard-nosed, inflexible ASOC environment, however, I fear many would have departed to avoid being beaten into submission. Those that complied in lockstep would still be first-level supervisors, just cogs in the wheel."

The sentiments gained traction with the SISC leaders, finally leading to a successful campaign that returned a bit of sanity to ASOC. Sometime after that, the company fired BPINC. Officially, the company dismissed them because they provoked union uprisings throughout the company and could never again duplicate the excellent SISC results in other areas. Dan, of course, always took credit for starting the process with his rants.

Soon after BPINC's departure, Dan's staff called to confess they had mistakenly selected and announced a SISC in an adjacent state as the winner of the second annual "most improved" award. After officially publishing the rankings, they discovered a mistake in their arithmetic.

Graham's SISC had narrowly surpassed the declared winner to qualify for the second year in a row. Apologizing, they asked Dan's advice on how they should handle the embarrassing situation just one week before the formal recognition ceremonies at headquarters. Dan paused and reflected on a conversation he'd held with McKinney while working on his staff. Several years earlier, Steve related a story about receiving the most improved player award on his high school football team. This was at the end of his first (sophomore), year and his father was quite pleased. At the end of his junior year, McKinney attended another season-ending awards ceremony where he heard his name announced again. He was the most improved player for the second year in a row. Upon proudly displaying his trophy at home, his dad remarked, "Boy, you must have been some kind of *bad* when you started playing two years ago!"

Graham told his staff director to quietly ignore the error and give the award to his rivals.

10

Seven Unruly Guests and a Fond Farewell

Graham's management team had finally integrated the ASOC system into the fabric of the SISC and his daily challenges began to subside, but not for long. His state was about to endure visits from Charley, Frances, Ivan, Jeanne, Dennis, Katrina, and Wilma: seven hurricanes over two seasons. Any storm in the southeastern US would negatively affect operations in Graham's SISC since they had responsibilities across the entire state and assisted other SISCs in the southeast and gulf regions. In fact, his SISC absorbed a huge work volume from the devastated functions transferred from New Orleans and surroundings after Hurricane Katrina. During the two years, several of the storms personally affected Dan's workers and their homes too, but they had to remain on duty to support the recovery efforts for months.

When Hurricane Wilma finally hit Graham's area, two of Dan's SISC buildings were directly in its path. It severely damaged the homes of many of his employees and knocked out power and other utilities for weeks. Despite the direct hit, SISC workers reported to work immediately after the storm since they provided services critical to the recovery of telecommunications to state and federal agencies. As Wilma approached, Graham consolidated all workers to the one building hardened to withstand category 5 hurricanes and equipped with emergency generators. Having read about *servant leadership*, Graham realized this would be a perfect opportunity to practice the concept. Rather than demanding his people work the overtime and fend for themselves during the trying times, Graham and his management team arranged to truck in food and water from 250 miles away, ensuring his people had lunches as they worked twelve-hour days. He and his management team also brought in ice from distant cities so they could refrigerate their food at home. Also without power, local gas station pumps were not operational, so Graham assigned a couple of his second levels to drive pickup trucks over a hundred miles three times a week to purchase multiple containers of gasoline. They allocated enough gasoline so that each of his three hundred south division workers could get to and from work daily.

As the power outages continued, Dan was becoming even more concerned knowing that his emergency turbine generators had been running nonstop for nearly two weeks. As their fuel tanks approached the empty mark, Dan worked with his corporate support group to secure several thousand gallons of special fuel oil. Since it was not available locally, they arranged to have it shipped to the city's seaport and trucked to his facility. Everyone was in crisis mode as the tanker finally pulled into the building just hours before the tanks ran dry.

Looking back, Graham viewed those two years as both the most stressful and the most rewarding in his career. As the lieutenant governor shook his hand several months later, he cited Dan's outstanding service during those difficult times. Coming a long way from his struggles as a young manager judged too quiet and shy to succeed, his *quiet* but *effective* leadership style was actually being recognized in an award ceremony! The plaque he received said simply,

Daniel Graham
Telephone Industry Hall of Fame
Florida Telecommunications Industry Association
2007

Before Graham's retirement, the company announced a pending merger with one of the four remaining telecom giants. The telecom taking over his company soon revealed plans to dismantle the regional SISC groups and absorb them into multiple international centers throughout the globe. During the reorganization process, Dan attended a dozen meetings and conference calls to assist in a smooth transition. The receiving leadership group was notably condescending and reminded Graham to recall *who bought whom* every time he offered a suggestion for structuring the new centers. The coleader of his coordination committee was stationed in Pasadena and insisted on scheduling the calls at 5 p.m. her time, thus forcing Dan and his team to report at their normal 7 a.m. East Coast time, work all day, and then attend a conference call starting at 8 p.m. They were all lucky to get home by 11 p.m.

When Graham requested that she consider the East Coast time difference and cut them some slack, she responded, "No, it's more convenient for us holding it as scheduled. When you chair the weekly series next month, you can schedule it a bit earlier for your convenience."

Graham agreed.

The next month, Dan distributed the meeting announcement, stating, "We will start our conference call *promptly* at 7 a.m. Eastern Standard Time," and eagerly waited for the phone to ring. "Four a.m.? Are you serious?" the voice on the other end said.

Dan explained that *she* could schedule it at her convenience the next month if she wanted. After accepting her apology for the previous behavior, he reissued the meeting notice with a more realistic start time. Graham sat back one last time and realized, at least in that situation, he had come a long way from that timid young manager who began in the business some thirty-five years earlier. He smiled.

Offered a very generous executive buyout, Dan approached the bittersweet task of purging three and one half decades of files and personal memorabilia. On his last day, the TWA union's local president and a couple of stewards knocked on his door for a final visit. "We wouldn't say this in public, but we hate to see you go. We've had our differences, but you always kept your word. You treated our members well during the hurricanes. And we think you did a pretty good job of helping our folks leave with a little extra pocket change during all the ASOC crap. Here's a small token of our appreciation." The union representatives placed a lapel button on Dan's desk, shook hands, and left quickly.

After they left, Dan read the caption on the little pin. It said, "Proud member of Local 3102." As he approached his car later that day to leave for the last time, he started to check behind his tires and then caught himself. *No,* he thought, *not this time!*

A few minutes later, approaching the entrance ramp to I-95 for the final ride home, he began to reminisce. Recalling that old saying "Lead, follow, or get *out* of the way," he thought about all the times he had faced exactly those three options in his career. He remembered the challenges during the years he led his division through multiple hurricanes and all those reengineering projects. He mulled over the times he tried to practice good followership, knowing that effective leaders had to first learn to take orders before issuing them. He also couldn't help but recall how he was figuratively pushed aside by bosses who forced him to get *out of the way* so they could pursue their own agendas.

As he pulled into his driveway, he sat in his car for a few minutes and felt a slight grin forming. He still remembered that "quiet person" who often felt intimidated by bosses some three and a half decades earlier. But he also remembered how he learned and grew as he became more confident and competent. Of course, he also recalled the role that *pure old luck* had played in placing him in the right place at the right time.

In the end, he was content to know that his bosses, employees, and union counterparts had come to respect him for his ability to lead, to follow, and to get *out* of the away. But most important, they appreciated him for knowing when to push back against poorly conceived policies that foreshadowed disaster. Yes, he thought, he had learned precisely how to *get in the way!*

INDEX 1

Alphabetized List of Business, Leadership, and Management Topics Indexed by Chapter

Topic	Chapter
Discipline vs. punishment	5
Doctrine of completed staff work	8
Downsizing	7
Dyads-empowering work groups	5
Economies of scale	9
Education benefits and downside	8
Efficiency analysis	9
Employee satisfaction surveys	3
Empowerment	1
Escalating problems up the line	5
Exec expeditions and assessments	5
Executive focus on lower tasks	8
Failure to accept responsibilities	6
Finding a way to be noticed	2
Flavor of the week management	6
Force reductions	9
Force-load equations	8
Formal vs. acting authority	7
Grievances—union	9
Grooming for promotions	5
In-and-out group relationships	5
Incompetence	3
Inflexible control systems	9
Information is power	4
Intimidation	3
Job enrichment and enlargement	1
Labor union rules for "surplussing"	9
Leadership style vs. effectiveness	7
Listening skills	4
Low-hanging fruit concept	4
Manage by walking around	9
Management by objective	3
Management ranking systems	7
Managerial tactics and analogies	5

INDEX 2

List of Business, Leadership, and Management Topics Discussed in Each Chapter

Chapter		Topics
Introduction		Management theory misconceptions and the concept of *serendipity* in business
1 It's Not Rocket Science		Vertical hierarchies, corporate motivation techniques, tuition programs, job enrichment and enlargement, promotion strategies, workplace politics, becoming indispensable, rotational assignments, orders, commands, position authority, directing, coaching, empowerment, identifying the requirements to move up the corporate ladder
2 Twelve Ducks, One Tuck, and Three Squirrels		Learning the tenets of corporate culture, management coaching and empowerment, personal power vs. formal authority, on the job training, wasting time but looking busy, assignment of additional work for being too efficient, lack of contractual obligations for salaried workers, finding a way to excel and become noticed
3 "I Want This Fixed!"		Management by objective, unrealistic goals, micromanaging, intimidation, managerial bullying tactics, managing the boss, employee satisfaction surveys, promotions to level of incompetence
4 Babbling PUCs, Beepers, and Stickmen		Information is power, listening skills, poor multitasking, Pareto Principle, 80/20 rule, low-hanging fruit concept, worker soldiering and inefficiencies, undercover boss, designing workflows to purposely reduce efficiencies

Chapter		Topics
5 A Broom, a Pumpkin, and a Bunny		Work yourself out of a job, union grievance procedures, dyads-empowering work groups, in-group and out-group relationships, lack of contingency plans, success and luck, situational leadership, executive expeditions, leadership assessment, grooming for promotions, discipline vs. punishment, managerial tactics and analogies to effect change, managerial skills vs. leadership skills vs. technical-task skills, matrix management, command and authority, task orientation vs. people orientation, escalation of problems up the organization, avoiding micromanagement problems, personality testing using Myers-Briggs instruments
6 A Buddy, a Wheelbarrow, and Two Meltdowns		Failure to focus on tasks and responsibilities, unbridled ambition, "flavor of the week" management, decisiveness, making informed decisions without all the facts, Total Quality Management, reengineering
7 The Top Ten Jobs List		Poor communication, downsizing, formal authority vs. "acting" supervision, management ranking systems, leadership style vs. leadership effectiveness
8 A Chief, but Which Doctor?		Customer satisfaction and correlation to corporate policies, management development and evaluation programs, education benefits and downside, confidence in assignments and reassuring the boss, force-load equations, matching manpower to work volume, higher executive focus on lower level tasks, importance of communicating to the workforce as a top executive, doctrine of completed staff work, managing by exception, statistical process control, managing the boss, rewards for positive performance, problems with developing reward expectations, delegating down rather than up the

Chapter		Topics
		org chart, compliance with manager's orders vs. disobeying orders when necessary, placing colleagues in positions to assist, politicking for a job, showing self-confidence in promoting your skills and abilities for promotional consideration
9 The Whac-A-Mole Conspiracy		Economies of scale, offshoring, efficiency analysis, time and motion studies, scientific management, standard time intervals, workflows, cyclical work volume and inability to match due to labor rules, seasonal or discontinuous fluctuations in workload, whistle blowing, inflexible management and control systems, suppression of alternate management tactics, certification procedures, manage by walking around, importance of communication during stressful times, force reductions, labor union rules for "surplussing," union contracts and requirements, grievances, union pushback and threats, top-down management decrees
10 Seven Unruly Guests and a Fond Farewell		Management integrity and respect between union leadership and management, emergency management, coordinating in multiple time zones, servant leadership—supporting workers in times of need

Printed in the United States
by Baker & Taylor Publisher Services